GENESIS ALPHA

GENESIS ALPHA

RUNE MICHAELS

GINEE SEO BOOKS
Atheneum Books for Young Readers
New York ∎ London ∎ Toronto ∎ Sydney

Atheneum Books for Young Readers

An imprint of Simon & Schuster Children's Publishing Division

1230 Avenue of the Americas, New York, New York 10020

Book design by Mike Rosamilia

The text for this book is set in Aldine401BT.

Manufactured in the United States of America

First Edition

2 4 6 8 10 9 7 5 3 1

CIP data for this book is available from the Library of Congress.

ISBN-13: 978-1-4169-1886-8

ISBN-10: 1-4169-1886-8

To Kjartan
for his love, support, humor, panic treatment, and plot
rescues—and never-ending patience with "researching"
computer games

ACKNOWLEDGMENTS

Thank you to—

My editor, Ginee Seo, and her assistant editor, Jordan Brown, for all their brilliant insights, suggestions, good humor, and patient hand-holding.

My agent, George Nicholson, for his faith and encouragement.

Everybody behind the scenes at Simon & Schuster, whose names I may not know but whose hard work and enthusiasm I appreciate.

Pam and Sarah, first readers and first critics, for patiently following me all the way from the first draft.

Ola, who responded graciously to panicked, last-minute medical questions.

Þórunn, who provided helpful insights into cat midwifery.

Jón Bjarni and Sigrún, who gave me excellent feedback through critiquecircle.com, and Sara Elísabet, for being Sara.

And my family: Tristan and Tamíla whose purring keeps me sane, and Kjartan, who knows a million loving ways to tell me to stop whining and start writing.

GENESIS ALPHA

We were playing a computer game the day it happened.

Genesis Alpha. It's the greatest game ever invented, and it's huge, a whole universe filled with thousands of people from all over the world. It's got everything: space battles and swordfights, aliens and elves, planets and cities and underground systems. I can play for hours every day, especially when my brother Max joins me.

I play at home after school, Max from a computer lab somewhere on campus. He's older than me, and he's away at college, so mostly we keep in touch through the game.

We fought Kreepz that day. They had enslaved the entire population of Yartan 3. The slaves were kept in caves deep underground, mining precious metals from the earth. So there was a lot of treasure to be had, yartanite and black diamonds.

The underground cave system was huge, but apart from the big gangsters at the entrance, the Kreepz guards down below weren't all that tough. So we split up. Alezander—that's Max's character name—took care of the east side while I did the west side. Alezander had his Bloodstone axe, and I had my broadsword. That's the coolest thing about Genesis Alpha. You can fly around in a spaceship and run around cities with a machine gun, but when you go down on a primitive planet, you wear old-fashioned chain-mail armor and wield a sword or a crossbow. It's got the best of all worlds.

I shot through the tunnels, killed a lot of Kreepz, and opened any locked doors I came across, freeing the slaves. They thanked me and rushed off, out of the caves and toward freedom. I emptied out the whole area, filling my bags with stuff. Then I went back to the entrance, still littered with the bones of the gangster Kreepz, and waited for Alezander.

We always split everything even. That's how Max wanted it, although it really would be fair that he got the bigger half because he's been playing Genesis Alpha longer and his character is bigger and stronger than mine. But Max always said it was too much bother, so we'd just put the loot in one big pile, pick out any good items we wanted to keep, sell the rest, and split the cash.

Alezander never returned.

He was still online, but he didn't respond when I sent him an instant message. So I returned into the caves to search for him.

Alezander was standing still in one of the guard cells, surrounded by Kreepz bones, and one small Kreepz was hitting him but not doing any damage. I quickly finished it off and then checked out Alezander.

Alezander was there, but Max wasn't. If you turn off your computer without logging off first, you freeze inside the game, like a statue, and if you don't return to the game quickly, moss starts growing on you. It's really funny. If you stay away a long time, the statue gets splattered with bird droppings and graffiti and eventually starts to crumble. No moss had started growing on Alezander yet, but his eyes had frozen; he no longer blinked. So I knew he'd been disconnected.

I wasn't worried. It's not like it had never happened before. Max would have friends come over and drag him away from the computer and he would just hit the off button, wouldn't even spare the time to say good-bye. Or he'd be playing in class and suddenly have to hide what he was doing from the teacher. It's really frustrating when he drops off without warning when we're in the middle of something important, and this time we'd planned to use the treasure from this mission to raise some cash for more mines and ammo, then fly directly to another place, Toxic Mountain, where we had unfinished business from last weekend.

Not today. I kicked Max's statue and went back to my spaceship for a solo mission.

A couple of hours later the phone rang. Downstairs, Mom answered.

And everything changed.

"My God, Max, what happened?" Mom yelled into the phone, loud enough to carry upstairs and into my room despite the closed door, loud enough to break through my concentration. Max hardly ever phones home and Mom hardly ever yells, so I knew right away something was

3

wrong. I ran out of the ruined city with a horde of mad Milas shooting at me, jumped into my spaceship, and locked it up. Then I made my way out of my room to the top of the stairs, listening.

Mom was standing at the old desk by the kitchen, where they keep an old-fashioned phone, with a rotary dial and everything. She said something to Max, but I didn't hear. Dad appeared at the door to the kitchen, holding his favorite mug. Max got it for him for Father's Day once. It has a picture of Freud on it, and it says "Sometimes coffee is just coffee. Except when it's tea."

"What?" Dad asked when he saw the look on Mom's face. A few drops sloshed over the rim of the mug as he hurried over to her. "What's going on? What's wrong?"

Mom shook her head at him and turned away, hunching over the phone. "Max" was the only thing I could make out. She talked urgently, but her voice was too low to carry. Then she hung up and put both hands on the desk, leaning over it as she took deep breaths.

"What? Laura, what did he say?" Dad asked. I inched toward the stairs. "Is Max okay?"

"I don't know," Mom said faintly.

"What did he say?"

"He's . . . he's been . . . arrested."

I gasped. One time Alezander got locked up in a prison cell on the Dak colony. I nearly got killed before the militia guards surrendered, but no explosives worked on that door. I had to pay a fortune for special bioengineered lock picks.

Dad's mug rattled as it hit the table. "Arrested? For what?"

"I don't know. He didn't say. He didn't say anything. He sounded . . . so scared and confused. He said to get him a lawyer." Mom clutched her head with both hands, looking wildly up at Dad. "Do we know a lawyer?"

I went with them to the police station. I didn't ask permission, just followed them and sat in the back of the car, silent. It worked. They knew I was there, but they were too busy thinking about Max and didn't bother telling me to stay behind.

"What could it be about?" Mom said. She was sitting in the passenger seat. Mom tends to drive too fast under normal circumstances, so when she's upset it's not a good idea for her to drive at all. "Drugs, Jack? Do you think he's doing drugs?"

Max, doing drugs? I grinned at the thought, and I must have made a sound because Dad frowned at me in the rearview mirror. But it was funny. Max doesn't even drink, he never has. He thinks it's stupid to ingest something that makes your mind go all weird. He says he wants to be in control of his own brain, all the time.

Then we got to the jail and nothing was funny anymore.

Max has been in custody three weeks now. That's almost a month.

A lot can happen in a month.

Like my birthday, not that anyone noticed. I'm thirteen now.

I was twelve when the girl died.

5

Back when it all started, I was one of ten.

Well—it might have been nine. Or seven. Or eleven. I don't know.

But one of ten sounds good, so that's what I've always imagined.

Ten embryos, three days after the gametes—my mother's egg and my father's sperm—had merged inside a test tube. Ten clusters of maybe eight cells in a petri dish in a sterile white laboratory, filled with people in white coats hunched over scientific equipment.

They were looking at me.

Me, and my nine sisters and brothers—only not really brothers and sisters because they were only undifferentiated cells, not people yet.

I always imagine my mother being one of the people in the white coats, because she is a biologist, and she worked at that lab. But she wasn't. She was at home, filled with hormones and anxiety, waiting for me, hoping for me.

I know how it happened. I've read about it, and Mom has explained, and I see it so clearly in my head that it's almost like I was there.

Well, I *was* there. I just didn't have eyes or hands or a heart or a brain or anything yet. I was only a small bubble of DNA.

The biologists removed one cell from each of us, teased one cell away from the others. They put each tiny cell through genetic tests, examining the nucleus carefully, checking if any of us matched my brother. The scientists were my mother's colleagues—her friends—and they knew how important this was. So they must have been excited to find me, probably smiled down at me through the electron microscope, thrilled with being able to help my mom.

So they let me grow some more and then they put me inside my mother's womb. My cells kept multiplying, and I became more than an embryo. My heart and brain started to develop, I got elbows and toes and webbed fingers and a tail. Later I lost my tail, grew eyelids and fingerprints, I breathed water, sucked my thumb and got hiccups that made my mother laugh at Max's bedside, his eyes wide as Mom placed his hand on her stomach and he felt me kick into his palm.

At eight months—eight instead of nine, because my brother couldn't wait any longer—they cut my mother open, and I was born, a whole baby, a person. My brother's savior.

I saved my brother's life the day I was born. Minutes after I was pulled into the world, they took the blood from my umbilical cord, then they extracted the stem cells and injected them into him, to replace the cells that had already been killed by chemotherapy and radiation.

It worked. My cells cured him. It's been thirteen years, and he's not sick now, he doesn't have a deadly disease, he's alive and healthy.

Without me, he wouldn't exist. Without him, I wouldn't exist.

That makes us more than brothers.

Two

We sat in a waiting room with peeling yellow paint. We sat in an office with police detectives asking questions. They questioned me too, lots of questions about Max, what we did together, which games we played, who his friends were, until Dad got up and yelled that we'd better get a lawyer for us too. By that time the reporters had found out, but Max's lawyer found us a back exit, so we got out of there okay.

There's silence in the car on the way home. It's late and we're all exhausted yet so wired, the atmosphere vibrates with tension.

We didn't even get to see Max.

I stare out the window at the shadows dancing on the sidewalk, and I start thinking about the view from my booster seat, back when I was little. I loved to pretend I was bigger and sit in the regular seat, even though that meant I barely saw out the window and would get carsick. Sometimes Max let me switch with him, and our parents wouldn't notice, or they would act like they didn't notice. I loved that. I'd sit there, pretending to be a big kid, straining to see out the window, while Max would hunker on my booster seat, his head almost touching the ceiling, and whenever our eyes met we'd grin, knowing we were sharing a secret right there behind our parents' backs. It was a silly game, but we liked secrets. I loved sharing a secret with my big brother.

I can't believe this is happening to us.

I know what Max is accused of. When the girl was found, it was all over the news for ages. I know her name, I've seen her smile and laugh in home movie clips shown on television, and I know what happened to her. She lived not far from here, and when they found her body, a couple of months ago, it was a huge story.

It can't be true that Max did that. You have to be evil to do something like that.

If Max were evil, I would know. It can't be possible to live with someone, to grow up with someone, and not know they're that evil.

If Max were evil, when would it have happened?

In the second grade? The seventh grade? In high school? At college?

What makes people evil?

I can't think of anything that would turn a good person into a bad person, so I begin to wonder if some people are simply born bad. Then I start seeing babies in my head, crawling around with knives in their hands and evil sneers on their chubby faces, and that seems ridiculous too.

It's impossible. It has to be a mistake. Evil is something nameless, faceless, something dark and sinister and alien.

Or something ugly and twisted, like the monsters I meet in Genesis Alpha. Evil can't be something that lives in your house, that smiles and laughs and always find you the coolest birthday present.

Mom and Dad are talking in the front seat, fast and furiously. About lawyers, the press, a plan, a strategy, and I hear them both take deep breaths, and they frequently remind each other not to panic. I lean my head against the cool window, close my eyes, and let their voices wash over me, my mind filtering out the words so I hear only the tone, like the rise and fall of a melody.

I'll have to play Genesis Alpha alone this weekend. Somehow that's worst of all. Max and I always play together weekends. It's a tradition. Saturday morning we wake up early, I at home, he at college, and we play from eight in the morning until two in the afternoon. Mom doesn't like how much time I spend online. She keeps trying to restrict my gaming time, but Max came up with this plan. "Teenagers like to sleep until noon," he told me, grinning. "Just let Mom think you're sleeping in, and she won't bother you. Use headphones so she won't hear the audio, and wear your pajamas. That way you can say you just woke up if they come bug you."

It's funny, because I remember the way Mom used to moan about how Max would sleep past noon if she let him, and for a moment I wonder if he was really playing computer games back then.

I clench my hands and want to punch the bad thoughts away. I don't know why they sneak into my head like this.

This is Max. My brother. He's the victim of some terrible police mistake. It could just as well have happened to me, or to anyone.

"You okay back there, Josh?" Dad asks, and Mom twists around in her seat to look at me.

I nod. "Sure. Just tired."

"It's been a long day," Mom says. "Tomorrow will be better." She tries to smile at me, her face stiff with anxiety. "You've been great today, honey. Very brave through all this, and I know it must be scary."

I pull a face at my half-invisible image in the window and want to tell them I'm not a little kid anymore. I know what happened to Karen Crosse—I've followed the news. It was horrible, and it was real, nothing at all like horror movies, when you know it's all fake. I'm used to that kind of violence, the fake kind. I've read books with blood and gore on every page and played computer games where brains splatter all over the screen.

I'm not a big fan of those, though. I prefer big adventure games with a story line as well as action, adventures, and lots of good and evil. When you first start playing Genesis Alpha, you're completely neutral. Not good, not evil. What you become depends on how you play the game, which decisions you make. The game forces you to choose. Sometimes you need to do evil things to get a special item or enter a place or something. Like in the quest to get the Seal of Fire, you need to break into a citizen's house, and if you can't sneak past the people in there, they'll attack you for breaking into their house and then you have to kill them if you want to finish the quest. So I've tried it plenty of times. I don't like it very much. It just feels wrong.

Alezander prefers being good too. He doesn't go around slaying wandering animals or peaceful citizens, like some people do. Just enemies or bad guys. I let out a breath as I realize how important this is. It's almost like evidence. If Max were a psychopathic killer, he'd like to do evil things, and Alezander would be evil too. But I guess the police wouldn't think that was good enough proof.

Cars line our street, like when someone's hosting a really big party, a wedding reception or something. As we turn into the driveway, faces fill the view.

Reporters. Behind them, neighbors, friends, strangers.

Dozens, maybe even hundreds of curious people.

Mom gasps. Dad curses. We drive into the garage. I stare out the back window as the garage door closes, marveling that none of the shouting people enter the garage with us. I guess they can't. There must be a law against it, and most people don't break the law.

Mom mutters as she leaves the car, hiccups, like she's sobbing. Dad slams the car door, pulls mine open, puts his arm around my shoulders as we follow Mom into the house. I hear the phones ringing and wonder what would happen if I went back out there, exposed myself to the reporters and the vultures. Would they tear me apart? I've often seen celebrities or politicians on TV, surrounded by a throng of reporters, pushing and shouting, and I've wondered what would happen if the person just stood there, not saying anything, just waiting, like a statue of a disconnected character in Genesis Alpha. Would they shout and jostle forever? Or would they eventually fall silent and wait to see if he'd say something—anything?

I guess I could give it a try now if I wanted to.

Mom and Dad stride around the house, pulling all the curtains. They don't turn on any lights. "The basement," Mom says, grabbing my arm when I pass her on the way up to my room. "Don't go upstairs yet, honey. They'll see you through the window. Let's not give them the satisfaction. They'll give up and go away."

"It's just our fifteen minutes of fame," Dad says when we've settled down in the basement where our home entertainment system is. There are no windows there. No phones, although from upstairs we hear the sharp beeping of several. Our three house phones. Our cell phones, too. Even mine started ringing nonstop back at the jail. I switched it off.

Mom is crying. Dad is silent. He has his arm around her, but he's not saying anything to comfort her. That's strange. Dad rarely runs out of words. He's a college professor, and he loves to teach. He talks all day, and then he comes home and talks some more.

"We'll get this straightened out," he says at last. "Let's not go to pieces. Max needs us."

Mom digs a tissue out of her pocket, one of many she ripped out of the tissue box on the police detective's desk. She blows her nose. "You're right. Max needs us."

"The lawyer will fix this. You heard what they said—they have no real evidence. Of course they don't. It's all circumstantial—the poor kid was in the wrong place at the wrong time. They can't hold him for long. With any luck we'll have him home tomorrow."

Mom nods. She looks around. "Could be worse," she says philosophically, and I realize after a few seconds she's talking about the house, not Max's situation. The police had a warrant. They were at our house while we were gone. Searching for evidence that Max did what they say he did.

I ignore Mom's shout not to leave the basement and run up to my room. The door is ajar, and I never leave it open. I always shut the door when I'm gone, to keep the cats out. I don't mind them there when I'm at home, but if I'm gone, they can mess with my computer, knock the cables free or walk on the keyboard. Click once managed to shut down Genesis Alpha when I was in the middle of a mission, his paws hitting just the right keys. Ever since, the cats are not allowed on my desk.

I push the door wider, look around. My room is always messy. Very messy. Max would shake his head when he was home from college. Max is neat. He's organized. I'm not, and Mom keeps moaning over the state of my room, comparing it to Max's room when he was my age. I don't mean to be messy. It just happens that way, and it just seems so much trouble to keep things in order. Even when I try to be neat, my room turns chaotic all by itself.

I step inside, and I notice dust. Not ordinary dust. Gray

powder sprinkled on my desk, my keyboard, my windowsill, the door. Everywhere. Fingerprint dust.

I sag against the door when I see the state of my room, and it drifts shut at my back. They've gone through everything, they've put their filthy hands on everything I own. They've opened my drawers, flipped through my magazines, rifled through my clothes, lifted up my mattress. All my secrets must be in a police file by now.

My gaze falls on my desk. The keyboard is there. The monitor is there. The mouse, my headphones, the speakers.

Useless.

Below the desk there's an empty space, a rectangle of darker carpeting.

They've taken my computer. The police have seized my computer.

My heart speeds up at the thought of what this means. I'll miss out on tonight's battle. We've been planning an organized attack on the Blue Bandits gang all week, making detailed plans about who does what and when. My friends expect me there, they're counting on my new Nasarus battle cruiser with the cloaking device, they're counting on me to do the reconnaissance. I'm the only one who can properly stealth, and now I'll let them all down.

Sudden rage boils in my chest. I'm furious at Max.

But it's not his fault.

I push open the door to Max's old room, balance on the threshold as I look around, feeling dizzy when I see the devastation. It's been ripped apart even worse than my room. They've left his computer magazines in a mess on the bed, torn his movie posters down, pushed the furniture away from the walls, even cut his mattress open.

His old computer is gone too, of course. Not that it makes a difference. It's four years old and probably wouldn't be fast enough for Genesis Alpha.

I trudge back downstairs. There's nothing for me in my room now that my computer is gone. Just to be sure, I check Dad's study. It's supposed to be Mom's office too, but she doesn't use it often. She says she prefers to leave work behind at the lab.

Their two computers are gone too.

My parents are still in the basement, together on the sofa, their arms around each other. I keep my mouth shut about the mess upstairs and throw myself into an easy chair in the corner, where Mom used to read to me when I was little. Max would sit there when we watched TV on weekends, just the two of us. He'd sit in the chair and I'd lie on the floor in my pajamas, and if I started to doze off, he'd turn up the volume until I woke up again.

"How can they believe he did this?" Mom whispers. She's staring at Max's picture hanging on the wall. His high school graduation picture. "Max . . . our Max. How could they suspect him of something like this?"

"It happened. Someone did it."

Mom's hands push into her face, her knuckles burrowing into her eyes. "Of course *someone* did it. But we're talking

16

about Max, Jack. Our little boy. Do you know what that murderer did? How could anyone think Max would ever do something like that?"

"They don't know him like we do. All they know is that someone did it. Someone's son. Someone's little boy."

"Not our son!" Mom yells. Dad holds up a hand and she lowers her voice, but not by much. "Monsters come from bad homes, from bad people, they're bad seeds . . . None of that applies to Max! How can they think that? We gave him a good home, we raised him well . . . he was always a good boy."

Dad opens his mouth, and I hold my breath, only breathe again when he closes his mouth without saying anything. Dad is notorious for always playing the devil's advocate, getting everybody riled up because they think he has strange views. He always has to see many sides of each story. This time, that's a bad thing. "Of course," he says. "Of course he's innocent. I just meant that they can't know." He shrugs. "I mean, every family thinks their own is innocent."

"Well, he is. Max is innocent. A person who does something like this—it has to be a psychopath. Okay. Let's just examine that. There are signs, aren't there?" Mom is on her feet again, pacing. "Of psychopaths? There are some signs in childhood."

"Yes. The triad. Bed-wetting. Setting fires. Cruelty to animals."

"Max did wet the bed for a long time, but he was ill. That doesn't count. He never set fires."

"He liked to play with fire. He loved to play with matches, remember?"

"What child doesn't go through a phase like that? He never set fires without permission."

"Right."

"He never hurt animals."

"No, not that we know of."

Mom breeds Abyssinian cats. We've had cats and kittens in the house as long as I can remember. There's always at least one in every room. Or maybe it just seems that way because they tend to follow us around. They like company.

Mom scoops Click from the floor, hugs him too tight. "What do you mean, 'that we know of'?" Her voice rises hysterically. "What do you mean, Jack?"

"Nothing. I meant nothing." Dad exhales noisily. "I'm sorry. I keep saying the wrong thing right now, I don't know what's wrong with me."

"Max loves the cats. Our very first cat was for him. Remember? He'd wanted a pet for so long, and when he was in remission, healthy enough to enjoy it, we finally got him one. He loved that cat. Remember? Remember how devastated he was when Moritz died?"

Dad nods. "It will be okay, Laura. You heard what they said, it's just circumstantial evidence. They have no real proof. All they need is someone to step forward with an alibi, and Max will be released. Even without that, they don't have enough to hold him for long. He'll be fine. Everything will be fine."

Click has escaped from Mom. He jumps into my lap, settles down there, and starts to purr. My parents keep talking, and most of the time they don't seem to notice I'm even here. They know I'm here. I'm not hiding. But they don't notice me. They try to include me in the conversation, pat me on the shoulder when they notice me, but then the attention drifts off me and back to Max. I think that's how it will be until things are back to normal, until Max is back at college and the real killer is in police custody. Max has grown. He's locked inside a cell, but he's here too, filling every square inch of our minds.

Mom's staring at another picture now, hanging beside the graduation photo. Max, when he was sick, just before I was born. He was dying. They didn't know if he could wait for the cure, if he could survive until I was born, but he hung on, day by day. I gave Mom a hard time for months. She felt weak and nauseated and tired. Sometimes she and Max would be throwing up together. She needed sleep, and she couldn't always stay with Max overnight, like she'd done so often before. But whenever she said good-bye to him and went home to bed, she was terrified she'd never see him again.

He's white in the picture. As white as the bedclothes he's lying in. There's no hair on his head, and he's thin, so his face looks old. He's got big circles under his eyes, and he looks exhausted.

Max hates that picture. Mom and Dad like having it around to remind themselves of the miracle. The miracle of Max's cure. They used to have it upstairs in the living room, next to a picture of Max a year later, healthy. But Max hated it, and one day he tore up the picture. Mom had another made and kept it in their bedroom instead. When Max went off to college, the picture went up on the basement wall. They take it down and put it in a drawer whenever they're expecting Max home, but he knows about it. Sometimes they forget to take it down, or he comes home unexpectedly. He hasn't torn it up yet, though. He leaves it alone, but he doesn't like it.

"If Mom and Dad want to remember that time, fine," he once said in disgust, staring at the frame. "I don't see why. It was horrible." He walked closer to the picture, reached out to take it but hesitated. Then he gestured at the picture instead of touching it. "I feel like that person died, you know. He's not me. He's just a sick little kid who died in that hospital bed and never grew up."

"Don't you remember?" I asked.

Max looked at me, but kind of through me, like he was thinking about something else. "Yes, I remember. I remember lying there and thinking about death. They'd explained it to me, you know. Death. Because I knew I was dying. They tried to keep it from me, but I'd known for a long time there was very little hope. When I wanted to know what would happen to me after I died, they told me I'd go to heaven." He shook his head. "Imagine that."

"Weird," I said. It's weird because our family is not religious.

Max shrugged. "I guess they thought it would be too cruel to tell a little kid he would be buried in the ground, disappear into dust. So they gave me the gift of religion." His voice was heavy with irony. "Then you came along, Josh. You were better than religion. You cleansed me. They killed all the bad stuff inside me and replaced it with your perfect little baby cells. It was poison, you know. The chemotherapy, the radiation. They gave me poison, so they'd kill as much of me as they could without killing me off entirely, and I got your cells instead of mine."

"They killed the cancer. Not you."

"The cancer. And a lot of other stuff with it. My hair, for one thing. And who knows what else? That's why I was so sick most of the time. It wasn't because of the cancer itself, it was the chemo and the radiation. It didn't cure me, and it just left me more sick." He shrugged. "Sometimes I wonder why they bothered."

"The treatment slowed the cancer down. Else you'd have died before . . . before they found a cure," I said, feeling like I was defending myself, justifying my existence.

Max laughed. He grabbed me in a rough hug, his arm tight around my shoulders as he ruffled my hair. "You're right, Josh. And they found me a cure. They found me you. Thank you."

Three

The next morning, when I open my eyes, everything is normal for a moment. Like always, I wake two minutes before the alarm clock rings and stare up the ceiling, wondering how long it takes two minutes to pass this time. It's not always the same. Sometimes two minutes pass in a flash, sometimes they take forever.

So for a little while the world is the same as always and the seconds tick by. Then I remember nothing is normal anymore, and the world tilts upside down and I'm in my bed, looking down at the ceiling and feeling dizzy, wondering where Max is right now and what kind of a ceiling he's looking at.

Still, there's school, even in a world where nothing makes sense, so when the alarm goes off, I drag myself out of bed and get dressed. Go downstairs where Dad sits at the kitchen table. His hand is wrapped around his coffee mug like always, but instead of the morning paper, he's reading a scientific journal. Or rather, pretending to read. I see he's only pretending because there's nothing but ads on the open pages.

"Morning, Josh," he says when I sit opposite him. He flattens the journal so the spine creases and the journal stays open. He pushes his glasses up on his nose and looks at me. "How are you coping this morning? Could you sleep?"

I make a face, like always when Dad uses shrink-speak on me. Which happens on a regular basis. Like every day, even when my big brother hasn't just been accused of a terrible crime. "I'm fine, Dad." I reach for the cereal and dump a small portion in my bowl, as small as I think I can get away with. Dad gets on my case if I don't eat breakfast. He keeps telling me the brain thrives on glucose, and that it's so needy it uses twenty percent of the energy we consume. I must be the only kid in the world to get a neurochemistry lecture every time I try to skip breakfast. "Your brain needs glucose," Dad will yell as I run past the kitchen. "Don't you dare leave the house without breakfast!"

"But I'll miss the school bus," I'll whine, but Dad will just point to a kitchen chair.

"You'll miss more than that if your brain is running on empty. Eat!"

In short, my dad's a total breakfast nazi. My brain needs glucose, but I'm not allowed to eat sugarcoated cereal for breakfast. Go figure. I glance around for the morning paper— I usually steal the middle sections from Dad, just to give my eyes something to do while I shovel the cereal into my mouth—but it's nowhere to be seen.

"You might as well go back to bed if you like," Dad says, and I look up. "I already phoned your school and told them you wouldn't be in today."

"Huh?" It's hard to be articulate with a mouthful of dry cereal.

Dad slams his palm down on the journal, clenches his fist. He pulls the morning paper from the floor at his feet, slams it on the table. "There is no way I can protect you from this, Josh. I wish I could, but I can't."

I look. Max's picture, on the front page. Not surprising, but still weird to see his face there.

· Then I see it.

My picture.

My picture.

Taken yesterday, though the window of our car.

I stare at my own grainy face for a while before my eyes are drawn to the headline: DESIGNER BABY SAVED KILLER'S LIFE.

Oh, boy.

I pull the paper closer for a better look. The article is long. It continues inside the paper. I glance at the subheadings, and it's pretty predictable, nothing I haven't seen before. The ethics of designer babies. The risks of playing God. Max's arrest is new fuel for those who think I shouldn't exist—if I hadn't been "created," a killer wouldn't be alive—and Karen wouldn't be dead.

"There was a reason this man got sick as a child," someone says in an interview, speaking of my brother. "It was part of a divine plan. And we interfered. We slapped the hand of God when He reached out to save this girl. . . ."

So it's my fault.

I stop reading. Push the paper away, and Dad takes it,

tosses it on the chair with the rest of this week's papers, ready for the recycle bin.

"I'm sorry." Dad rubs his hands over his face. He looks tired, like he hasn't slept. "So you see, it's probably not a good idea for you to go to school today. Not with all this mess going on and the press on our case. I already talked to the principal—she's going to have your teachers e-mail you assignments this week."

I groan. "Aw, Dad! What's the point of skipping school if I still get homework?"

A ghost of a smile touches Dad's mouth. He ruffles my hair, and like always, I twist my head away, and he pats my shoulder instead.

"What about practice? Can I at least go to baseball practice?"

Dad shakes his head. "Not a good idea, Josh."

"What about my friends? Can I go to their houses? Can they come over?"

"I don't know. We'll have to play it by ear. See what happens."

"When can I go back to school?"

"Next week, I hope. Maybe this will have blown over by then. We have private investigators working. They'll prove Max's innocence. But we're not going to work today." Dad takes a deep breath. "We both got a few days off. Lots to do. We're seeing Max today. Short visit, supervised, but at least we get to see him."

"Can I come?"

Dad hesitates. "Would you want to?"

"Of course! I've never seen the inside of a jail."

Dad groans.

"I mean, I want to be there for my brother," I amend. Oops. Fortunately, Dad doesn't mind ulterior motives. He says it's mental multitasking, a sign of intelligence—even if it's not always *nice*. "It just so happens that I'd also like to see the inside of a jail."

Dad shakes his head. "Not this time, Josh. We only have permission for the two of us. Maybe next time," he adds when I scowl in frustration. "I'm sure you can find something to do while we're gone."

No school. No homework yet, so I'm free. I can spend the whole day playing Genesis Alpha. I'll play alone though, since most of my local friends will be at school, but some of the foreigners will be there, it's already afternoon in Europe and evening in Australia and Japan. I munch on cereal while I calculate time zone differences and anticipate an uninterrupted day of space travel—and then I remember. My computer is sitting in an evidence room somewhere, being poked and prodded by forensic experts. In fact, there isn't a single computer in the house.

I feel like screaming, but instead I bang my fist on the table, making Dad jump.

"What?"

"My computer, Dad! I can't get into Genesis Alpha without my computer!"

"A day or two without Genesis Alpha. That's indeed a catastrophe."

"Yes! It is! I've got plans, people are counting on me. . . . When do I get my computer back?"

"I have no idea. Soon, I hope. It's not like they'll find anything. I'll ask someone today if I can."

"What am I supposed to do until then?" I whine.

Dad looks at me dryly. "I don't know, Josh. Camp out in front of the TV like we did back in antiquity? There are a million books in this house. The cat shed always needs a good cleaning, and if you're really bored, I'm sure we can find lots of chores."

Dad always makes good on threats like that. "I'm cool," I say quickly. "Where's Mom?"

"In the study. Diane's here, they're talking."

Diane Ashe was one of Mom's colleagues, back when she worked in the genetics laboratory. She helped Mom get pregnant with me, so she's Mom's big hero. She saved Max and gave me to Mom and Dad. So in return, my brother and I were her guinea pigs. Dr. Ashe got access to both of us for all sorts of tests and stuff, usually once a year, around my birthday. Last time I refused to participate, and Max dropped out ages ago. Mom wasn't pleased. She says Max and I both owe Dr. Ashe our lives, and the least we can do is help her with her research.

"What's *she* doing here?"

Dad scolds me with a look. He knows I don't like Dr. Ashe, and I think he even understands why, but he doesn't approve when I show it, and he yells when I call her Dr. Die-Hard, the nickname Max invented. But then he's not the one she stares at like something under a microscope. When she looks at me, I feel like she's still seeing a cluster of transparent cells, like she still has the power to flush me down the toilet or tip me in the trash.

"Diane is our friend, Josh. She's known both you and Max forever, and she's just as distressed about this as we are. She's hoping she can do something to help. She even offered to stay with you today."

I straighten up in alarm. "No!" If anything was worse than a day without Genesis Alpha, it would be a day with Dr. Die-Hard instead.

Dad chuckles wearily. "I know, Josh. Don't worry. She'll be leaving with us."

I slump in relief. "Phew. Thanks, Dad. Nice save."

Dad puts his elbows on the table and rests his chin on his hands. "Josh—how are you feeling?"

That's my dad. His older son is in prison, accused of one of the most horrible crimes there is, and he's settling down to a therapy session with *me*.

"I'm okay."

Dad leans over and retrieves the newspaper. He pushes it closer, right under my nose, so I can't avoid seeing our pictures. Max and me, side by side, two mug shots. "Are you okay with what they're saying here?"

I glance at the headline. "That they're blaming me, you mean? Max didn't do anything, so that cancels it out, doesn't it?"

Dad holds my gaze in that way he does, not allowing me to look away. "Yes. But if he were to do something terrible someday, how would that make you feel? Would you feel responsible in some way, because you saved his life?"

The question nibbles at the edges of my thoughts, but I don't allow it any closer, because it doesn't matter. It isn't relevant. Max hasn't done anything bad.

"Because that would be absurd, wouldn't it, Josh? There's a difference between being responsible for your own actions and taking responsibility for something that you had no control over, something you couldn't possibly predict or do anything about. Isn't there?"

"I guess," I mutter, and stuff my face with what's left in the cereal bowl to avoid another in-depth philosophical debate with Dad. I suppose there is a difference. But then you'd have to be able to tell which is which.

When Mom and Dad are gone, I have nothing to do. Out of habit I trudge upstairs and sit down at my desk, stare at my useless monitor and think about all the things I could be doing in Genesis Alpha right now. I could explore. Fight. Go on missions or solve quests. Play the stock market or trade. Chat and just hang out with aliens from all corners of the galaxy.

Instead I'm stuck on planet Earth without a spaceship.

I throw myself on the sofa in front of the television and flip between channels for a while, but nothing really catches my attention. I go through our movie collection, but there's nothing there I want to watch either. I take a nap, glance through the paper, play with Click for a while, and finally, in desperate boredom, I grab the vacuum cleaner and get rid of most of the fingerprint dust from my room.

The phones keep ringing all day, but they're set on mute, so as long as I don't look at that blinking red light on the answering machine they don't bother me. The caller ID tells me when it's someone I know, and Mom calls once, Dad twice, to check how I'm doing, but there's no news, at least none that they're telling me. The moment school is out, I can't take it anymore. I call Frankie.

"Wow, this is huge!" is the first thing he says. I hear noise around him. A lot of echo. He's probably passing through the main hall on his way out of school, and I wish I were there. If I could go to school, I might be able to sneak into Genesis Alpha for a few minutes using the library computers. I'd at least be able to post on a message board, let everyone know I'd be out of commission for a few days. "They're talking about you all over school, man," Frankie continues. "Everybody's asking about you and Max."

I roll my eyes. I'm curious about what they're saying, but I'm not sure I want to hear it. "Well, they pulled me out of school for now. I'm stuck at home for a while. Maybe all week. I can't even go to baseball practice or anything."

"That sucks. Hey, I'll come over. I can be there in ten."

"Okay. But take a shortcut through the backyard," I tell him. "In case the press is still hanging around. They were all over our street yesterday."

"They don't scare me," Frankie says. He hangs up, and ten minutes later the doorbell rings.

Frankie's back is to me when I open the door. He's cran-ing his neck in all directions. "No press," he says, sounding disappointed when he shuffles inside. "They were at school today, you know. Two of them, hanging out outside the gates. They asked us loads of questions until the principal ordered them to keep their distance or she'd call the police. Were the police here? The news said they got a search warrant for your house and everything."

Frankie sounds way too excited about this whole thing. I want to tell him to shut up, but I clench my teeth and just shrug. "Want to watch a movie?"

"How about a couple of hours on Genesis Alpha?" Frankie asks. Sometimes he borrows Mom's computer and we both play at my house. "You missed a great battle yester-day. We nearly didn't make it, but Ace came through in the end. We got some great loot. I got an antique sword with a healing function. It's even better than yours."

"Wow."

"Why didn't you show? Were you busy with the police? Did they interrogate you and all? Are you in trouble too?"

I nearly growl. "Of course I'm not in trouble. But we can't play. The police took my computer. They took all the computers."

"The police took them? Oh man!" Frankie almost jumps from one foot to another, glancing in the direction of the stairs. "Can I, you know, peek into Max's room?"

"No! What for?"

"Just curious. You know . . . just curious."

"Well, no, you can't! Let's go to my room."

I lead the way up the stairs, although I've almost changed my mind about having Frankie here. I push open the door into my room, but Frankie isn't following me. I look back and see him in the doorway to Max's room. "Hey!" I yell. "I said not to go there!"

Frankie doesn't hear me. His mouth is open as he looks around. The room still looks like a war zone, and there's fingerprint powder everywhere.

"Wow," he whispers. "Were the police looking for fingerprints? What are they looking for? I mean—did he bring the girl here or something? He didn't actually do it here, did he?"

I kick him. Hard. It's a reflex, like when a soccer ball lands right in front of your foot, it just happens automatically. He jumps away and bends down, grimacing, rubbing his shin. "Ow! What the hell is your problem?"

"What the hell is *your* problem?" I shout. "You're talking about Max. Remember Max? My brother, the guy who used to fix our bikes when we were little? The guy we play Genesis Alpha with every week? He didn't do it! He didn't do anything wrong!"

"I just . . ." Frankie stutters. I clench my hands and want him gone. Want to drag him out of the room, punch him in the face and scream at him never to come here again.

But I've been alone all day and I'm sick of it, and if we could just stop thinking about Max and instead talk about Genesis Alpha or even school or something, everything would be okay. So I swallow my anger even though it's burning hot in my chest. "Come on. Let's watch a movie or something."

"Yeah, sure. Okay." Frankie has his back to me, still rubbing his shin. There's something strange in the way he's moving, and then I hear a tiny click.

His cell phone.

He's using it to take pictures of my brother's room.

Four

Cell phones are pretty sturdy. I've always been careful with mine, but obviously I don't need to be. Frankie's phone doesn't even crack when I hurl it from the top of the stairs to the tiled floor in the entrance. "Are you nuts?" Frankie yells. He shoots down the stairs and dives for it, and I do too, and then we are rolling on the floor, fists pounding, feet kicking, screaming and yelling so the house echoes with the sounds.

Nobody wins. Nobody loses either. After a while the fight sort of peters out and we're sitting on the floor, breathing heavily and staring at each other like we're mortal enemies.

"I can't believe I ever thought you were my best friend," I spit out at him. "A best friend wouldn't do something like that!"

"Okay, okay. I'm sorry. I'll delete the pictures." Frankie gestures at the phone, lying near the front door, a hairline fracture in its screen now from when I banged it against the floor while Frankie held my head against the wall and tried to twist my ear off. "If you don't trust me, you can do it yourself. Okay?"

I crawl toward the phone, not taking my eyes off Frankie, but he just sits there, wheezing after our fight. I flip through the photo file in his phone. He's taken three pictures, blurry and dim images of the chaos in Max's room, and I delete them all, making sure everything is gone from the deleted folder too. I slide the phone across the floor back to Frankie. He looks at it, stares at the cracked screen, but he doesn't say anything about it. "Sorry," he mutters. "I guess I shouldn't have. I just thought it would be cool . . . you know. Because everybody at school is asking me . . . I just . . . it's not like I'd planned to sell them or anything . . ."

"Jerk," I mutter, and I'm so angry I almost feel like crying. My shoulder hurts and my lip is throbbing. Blood is leaking down my chin. Frankie doesn't look any better, and Dad's going to have my hide for this. "You're such a jerk, Frankie. Max didn't do anything."

"Are you sure?" Frankie asks. "I mean, how can you be sure? They arrested him. They don't go around arresting people for no good reason."

"Go away!" I yell. "Just go away and leave me alone!"

Frankie leaves, and I don't know if he's ever coming back. I don't know if I ever want him to come back. We've been friends since kindergarten, and we've fought plenty of times, but usually we pretend nothing happened next time we meet.

I don't know about this time.

I'm alone again. Just me and the cats.

I like the cats, which is good, because I look after them a lot. I'm home from school earlier than Mom's home from work, so they're my responsibility for a couple of hours. Sometimes we have to hand-feed a kitten because it's too weak to suckle. Sometimes kittens die. There's a tiny kitten cemetery in the corner of our backyard. All our kittens get names, even the ones who are born dead. We carve every name into the side of the cat shed, in a sort of family tree. Mom's been breeding cats almost all my life, so that's a lot of names.

When it gets close to dinnertime, there's another message from Dad that they're not sure when they'll be home, and I should just throw something in the microwave for dinner. I get bored enough to go clean the litter boxes. The cats have the run of the house, but they have an outdoor cage, too. A cat-size tunnel leads there, and then they get to taste the wind and dig their claws into the grass inside the big wire enclosure. Their litter boxes are inside a waterproof shed, where we also keep the gardening tools and our bicycles and stuff. Mom thinks that's pretty ingenious. No nasty smells in the house.

The cats mostly use the outdoor cage in the summer. They don't like snow and rain much, so in the winter they only use the tunnel to get to their litter boxes. Mom pays me to clean them. It's not that big a deal, and the cats are curious and grateful. They gather around me while I work, and line up to use the boxes afterward.

Before Max left for college this was his job. He'd spend an hour out there every afternoon, cleaning up and playing with the cats. He was our family vet too. He'd read up on kitty problems online and stay up all night when they were about to give birth. Even after he went off to college, Mom called him for advice if there was a problem.

If Max were a monster, he wouldn't have been nice to the cats.

I put on my jacket and boots, open the back door. It hasn't snowed for a while, so there's still a worn path through the snow toward the shed from my last visit. I unlock the shed door and slip inside.

I like it out here. It's a nice place to be alone, especially in the spring and autumn, when it's not too cold and not too hot. I have an old MP3 player in the cupboard with the huge bags of litter, and there's an old mattress on the floor where I can lie with my eyes closed, listening to music with cats purring on my chest. I also keep a dartboard here, which I'm not allowed to have in the house. It was Max's originally, but he passed it on to me when I took over the shed. Mom would go nuts if she knew about the darts. She wouldn't trust us to be careful enough around the cats.

We have a battery-operated lamp in here, but I don't bother turning it on. There's still some daylight coming in through the grimy windows stretching along the ceiling. I get the trash bags out and kneel down to scoop cat poop, but then I freeze.

There's movement in the dark corner, where the old lounge chair is. Where I sometimes sit with a cat on my lap, holding on to a paw while I cut their claws.

There's someone there.

For an absurd moment I think it's Max, and fear flows through me, an electric charge zapping through my nerves. It's ridiculous, and I get furious at myself. I have no reason to fear my brother.

But my pulse, the blood pounding in my veins, the metallic taste in my mouth—my body is telling me something different. It's not fair. It's not right. My fear is a betrayal of Max. It's horrible. It's much worse than what Frankie did. Frankie is just a friend. Max is my brother. More than my brother. If I don't believe in him, who will?

I swallow. Anger balloons out to push away the fear and the suspicions, and even though the stranger is skulking in the shadows like a shy cat, I don't need to see who it is. I know it can't be Max.

"Who are you?" I bark, trying to sound scary. "What are you doing here?"

A cat jumps out of the shadows, startling me. It's Cleopatra, one of our three females. She's pregnant, due to give birth soon. She rubs against my ankles, purrs, then saunters toward the tunnel leading back to the house.

But she's not the only one in here. There's a human-size shadow in that corner, between me and the door. There's a smell here too, and I should have noticed it sooner. A human smell. Soap. Shampoo. It stands out against the cat smells. "Who are you?" I repeat. Is it someone from the press? Would they be crazy enough to trespass like this? I put my hand in my pocket, curl my fingers around my cell phone, pull it up, and press a button so the screen lights up. "I'm calling the police," I say, pressing 9 and moving my finger to the 1.

There's movement. A bored sigh. I glimpse a face. It's a girl. She's standing up. She brushes dust off her jeans, steps forward into the light straining through the narrow windows.

She looks my age, maybe a little bit older. She's wearing a hooded sweater, so I don't see her face very well, but I see the glint of her eyes as she looks at me arrogantly, like I'm supposed to recognize her. I don't. She does looks a little familiar, but I don't know why. She's definitely not anyone I know.

"Who are you?" I repeat. I still clutch the phone, but it feels stupid to be afraid of this girl. "This is private property. You're trespassing."

She doesn't answer.

"Are you with the press?" It's a silly question. She's just a kid.

"No."

Her voice hardly carries, but it's not shy. Just . . . barely there. She's wearing an unzipped coat over the hooded sweater, and she stands very straight.

"Who are you?" I ask once more. "What are you doing here?"

"You look like *him*," she says. Her voice is dark and flat. "You're Josh. *His* brother."

"Max. Yes. He's my brother."

"I read about you this morning. In the paper. I saw your picture. You're the designer baby."

I'm silent.

"He had cancer."

I cross my arms. "You're not exactly telling me news here, you know."

She tilts her head to the side. "You saved his life. He wouldn't be alive if it weren't for you."

"What are you doing here?" I trace the buttons on my phone with my thumb. "Who are you?"

She finally pushes the hood back. Her hair is blond, reaches just below her shoulders, her eyes are big and green. She's very pretty. Prettier than most of the girls in my class. "Your brother killed my sister."

I almost drop the phone. When I realize my hands are shaking, I stuff the phone away and put my hands in my pockets. Her tone is belligerent. Angry. Like she expects me to protest her accusation, and of course I will.

But now I know why she looks familiar. Her face resembles the face I know from the television screen and newspaper pictures. Karen. Karen was pretty too. I remember Dad saying that was why her murder got so much attention, why it even made national news. They like to put pretty faces on television, and Karen was a beautiful blond, blue-eyed girl someone killed.

Someone. Not my brother. Not Max.

"Max is innocent," I say. "He didn't kill anyone. It's a mistake."

She leans forward. "If you had never been born, my sister wouldn't be dead."

I shake my head. "It wasn't Max."

"You don't know that. You don't know anything," she spits out. "You just hope." She sits back down on the lounge chair. The legs scrape against the floorboards as she leans back. She looks around, pats her knee absently as if asking a cat to jump in her lap. But they're all gone now. It's almost dinnertime and the cats know it. They are inside, clustered around their bowls, waiting, but there's no one there to feed them.

I wonder if Mom will even remember them tonight.

"You look a lot like him."

She says "him" with loathing and disgust. Like Max is not human anymore, like he's lower than a sewer rat, lower than bacteria. I guess when you do what he's accused of doing, you leave the human race behind. You almost become another species.

"Yes. I look like him."

"He's a monster."

I don't answer. Shivers of fear are giving me goose bumps. She's wrong. I know Max is innocent. But I'm afraid I'll start to doubt him.

"I said, he's a monster!" The girl is back on her feet. She has moved closer, getting right in my face, and her voice is louder, her fists clenched and her face tight in fury.

"I heard," I say. I step back, not because I'm afraid or because I can't take her, but because I don't fight girls, and besides, if I get in a fight with Karen Crosse's sister, there will be trouble.

The girl unclenches her fists when she sees me back off. "Your brother will be dead too," she says. "He'll get the death penalty for what he did. They'll shave his head and barbecue him in the electric chair. Or strap him down on a table and pump him full of poison until his heart can't beat anymore."

She smiles when I gasp aloud. I hadn't thought about that. Hadn't thought about the death penalty. For split seconds, I've imagined what would happen if this went to trial and Max was somehow found guilty. I've imagined Max in prison forever, me visiting him when we were both old and gray and our parents gone.

But I never thought about the possibility of the death penalty.

"You'll get to say good-bye, though," the girl says. "We never got to say good-bye to Karen."

"You have to go," I say. "This is private property. You're trespassing."

The girl laughs. She walks toward the door. Opens it. Steps outside. She turns around and looks back at me, framed against the fading light outside. Snow has begun falling again and the flakes stick to her hair. "My sister was also private property."

Five

I'm in bed by the time Mom and Dad come home. The next morning they're preoccupied. Whispering to each other, whispering into the phone, occasionally forgetting and shouting instead. They don't even notice my swollen lip.

"How's Max doing?" I finally dare ask over breakfast. Mom rubs her face with her hands and pushes her bowl away.

"He's . . . holding up," she says. "It's not easy, but he's resilient. He always has been." She tries to smile at me. "He's asked about you."

"Can I go with you soon? Can I see him?"

"I don't know . . . Maybe. We'll see." Mom stands up, mumbles something about taking a shower and goes upstairs, her movements slow and dreamlike, like she's sleepwalking.

Dad grabs the remote and flips on the small TV we have in the kitchen. Max's face fills the screen, but the sound is muted after Dad stabs viciously at the remote. We stare in silence at Max's face, at Karen's face, a picture of our house, of Max's dormitory. Then finally they move to another story and Dad turns up the volume again.

Not quite another story, though. Another familiar face flashes on the screen.

"Rachel Crosse, sister of murder victim Karen Crosse, is missing."

I sit frozen, my spoon halfway to my mouth.

Rachel. Her name is Rachel.

"Rachel didn't come home last night, and she hasn't been seen since yesterday afternoon when she left school at around two o'clock. Rachel, fourteen years old, is five foot six, slim, with shoulder-length blond hair and green eyes. She was wearing jeans and a dark coat over a blue hooded sweater, and she was carrying a leather backpack."

I hear Mom come running back downstairs. There's hope and excitement in her face as she enters the kitchen. "I heard the news upstairs. Jack, did you hear?" She gestures at the screen. "If this girl has been killed too, that would be evidence. Wouldn't it? It would prove Max's innocence. They'd have to let him go and start searching for the real killer."

Dad looks at Mom, startled. "No. I don't think it would prove anything. Not in itself. Could be a copycat murder."

Mom deflates. Stops hoping Rachel is dead, I guess, and then looks ashamed when she realizes what she sounded like. "I didn't mean . . . oh, I hope they find the poor girl," she mutters. "To lose one child, especially like this, is a tragedy beyond words." She looks at me. "To lose another one the same way . . . it's unthinkable."

I finish my breakfast quickly, put my bowl in the dishwasher and head for the back door.

■ ■ ■

When I think about it, the cats have been very silent this morning. It's because they've been out in the cat shed, clustered around Rachel. She's found the closed cupboard where we keep the treats. She's sitting on the lounge chair, backed into a corner, and all five cats are there—on her lap, on her shoulders, nudging each other away at her feet. She digs into the treats bag, holds out palms full of goodies.

The litter boxes will be interesting tonight.

She looks up when I open the door, but she doesn't look worried. She makes eye contact only for a second, then turns her attention back to the cats. I stand there for a while, not sure what I'm doing—what she's doing, what either of us should be doing.

I should call my parents. I know I should, but I don't. There's enough trouble, and I guess I'm hoping this particular problem will leave of its own accord, without me having to get involved. So I walk toward her, grab the treats bag, tuck it away on a high shelf. The cats protest, but they soon forget about the bag and focus on getting the last treats out of Rachel's hands and nosing around her feet for leftovers. I sit down opposite her, silent until she looks at me defiantly. It's a trick Dad used to use on me. When he knew I'd done something I wasn't supposed to, he'd come into my room, sit down, and look at me until I broke down and confessed. Max tried to teach me tricks to resist it, but they never worked. Not for me. It's psychological warfare and Dad's a champion.

"What?" Rachel snaps at last. "Why are you staring at me like that?"

"Your name is Rachel."

"So what?"

"You were on TV. Your picture was on the local news. Your disappearance."

"Yippee. I'm famous. Not as famous as my big sister, though." Her voice sounds bored. Disinterested. She fishes around in the creases of her clothes, finds another cat treat or two.

"Your parents are freaking out. You have to go home."

Rachel shrugs. "I will. Sooner or later. Did you tell someone about me?"

I want to tell her I did, but it's obvious I didn't, or someone would be here. "No. Not yet."

She grins. "Why?" she asks, in a way that suggests she already knows the answer. Maybe she does. I don't.

"Go home, Rachel."

"No."

"Why?"

"None of your business."

"If you're hiding out in my home, that is my business. But fine. I'll just tell Dad. He'll deal with this." I stand up. Rachel does too. She puts her hands on her hips.

"You're not going to tell anyone." Her voice is ominous.

"Why not?"

"Because I said." She takes a couple of steps toward me. I blink, and suddenly she has a knife. She's holding it up between us, the sharp blade flashing, but I don't have time to be afraid before she's holding it out to me, the red handle first. "Here. Take it."

I take a step backward. It's just a Swiss Army knife, but it creeps me out. "No."

She moves closer, still holding out the knife. She moves it lower, toward my hand, tries to push it into my palm. "Try it, Josh. See how you like it. I bet you will."

I move my hands behind my back, take another step back and then another until I come up against the wall. I grab my left wrist tightly with my right hand. "Stop acting crazy!"

"Why? Am I scaring you?" She's grinning again. Her big green eyes seem to glow. "Your brother killed my sister with a knife just like this one. They're very popular, you know. You can buy one anywhere." Suddenly she brings the knife up to her face, touches it to her cheek. "He cut her here." She presses down, and a tiny drop of blood oozes up. "And that was just the beginning."

I'm breathing too fast, but I can't slow it down. I want to stop her, but I'm afraid to move, afraid to grab the knife, afraid something terrible will happen if I do, afraid something terrible will happen if I don't . . .

"You're crazy," I whisper as she pushes the knife deeper and a thin red line appears on her skin. I can barely hear myself, my heart is pounding so loudly in my ears.

"He cut her and cut her and cut her. Before he killed her. She bled for a long time before she died." She tilts her head to the side, as if asking me an important question. "Why? Why didn't he just kill her? Why did he have to hurt her first?"

"My brother didn't kill her!" Anger releases me from the paralysis of fear. My hand shoots out and I rip the knife from her. It's brand-new, with a million different functions, including a flash drive and everything.

The blade is streaked with red. I wipe it on my jeans. Then I crack the door open, raise my arm and toss the knife over the fence surrounding the shed, into the bushes at the edge of our backyard. I hear it thud into the ground. Rachel is looking at me when I turn around. Smiling. A drop of blood leaks down her cheek, curves toward her chin like a red tear.

"I've got you now." She's almost gloating.

"What? What are you talking about?"

"Evidence."

I don't understand what she means.

"I have a cut on my face. You have my blood wiped into your jeans. Out there's a knife with my blood and your finger-prints on it. And my fingerprints are all over this place. I can go to the police and say you kidnapped me, held me a prisoner here. That you attacked me with a knife just like your brother's. That you cut my face, just like he did to my sister."

I stare at her. She's still smiling.

"Or," she says, "you can kill me. You can kill me, get rid of my body, drag it out in the forest behind your house, and if you're careful, nobody would ever find out."

"What—"

"Except maybe you can't do that. Because maybe I've left

a note behind, telling everybody where I am and what must have happened to me."

"Why are you doing this?" I shout.

Rachel keeps talking. She's enjoying herself, I can tell. "So maybe I'll run away. Disappear forever. And they'll find the note I left, and the drops of blood on the floor here, and the traces of my blood in your clothes, and they'll think you killed me. They'll arrest you and question you and your face will be all over the papers. Again. Can't you picture the headlines? 'Blood Brothers.' And you and your brother will both go on trial for murder. After all, you guys are used to sharing cells."

"I'm telling my parents right now," I yell at her. "We'll call the police. Nobody will believe your crazy lies!"

I stalk out of the shed and slam the door shut, shaking. Rachel's laughter follows me. It's not a happy sound.

"Hey!" she calls. I pause. Turn around. She's standing in the doorway like she belongs there. She's even careful to leave the screen shut, like we always do so the cats can't get out. Her eyes glitter, and my spine feels cold. "Does your brother miss Genesis Alpha?"

Six

"Genesis Alpha?" I pause, sudden unease tingling inside me. "What do you know about Genesis Alpha?"

Rachel shrugs. She pushes her hands deep into the pockets of her jeans, turns around and disappears into the shed.

I heave the door open, follow her inside. "I asked you a question. What about Genesis Alpha?"

She settles down on the mattress. Cleopatra, the traitor, curls up next to her and starts to purr. "Maybe I'll tell you later. Maybe tomorrow—maybe not."

She's playing some stupid game, and I'm one of her pawns.

I refuse to beg. When she doesn't tell me, I shrug as if I don't care, and leave, slamming the door behind me.

I search for a long time before I find the knife. It has sunk through the layers of snow caught at the base of the bushes and is sticking up from the ground underneath. The snow has wiped the blade clean of Rachel's blood. I close it, put it in my pocket, and wonder what I'll do with it. I'm not even sure why I looked for it.

How does she know about Max and Genesis Alpha?

She doesn't. She doesn't know anything. A lot of kids play Genesis Alpha. Everybody knows about that game. Maybe she's even been spying on me, maybe she's been looking in through the windows and seen the Genesis Alpha poster on the wall in my room. She's just messing with my head.

I'm alone again, and the day is excruciatingly slow. I watch a lot of TV and ignore the phone, even though I'm going crazy, stuck inside like this. I try to focus on a science-fiction novel I'm reading, but it's hopeless. Even though I turn the pages and my eyes scan each line, I don't remember a word.

I wish I had my computer. Genesis Alpha can take my mind off anything, no matter how big and scary.

When Mom and Dad get home, they try to pay attention to me, ask about my day and stuff, but the phones keep ringing, and I can tell that they have trouble concentrating on anything I say. Everything revolves around Max, and I give up and get out of the way, go to bed early, sit up and read until finally the phones stop ringing. I don't know if people have stopped calling, or if Mom and Dad unplugged them.

"Josh?" Mom pushes my door open and peeks in. "You still awake, sweetie?"

"Yeah."

She comes in, sits on my bed, takes my book out of my hands, and scans the back. "Looks interesting," she says. "Is it?"

I nod. I don't really think Mom cares about colonization

of distant planets right now. "It's not bad. When can I go back to school?"

"Just a few more days, honey. I'm sorry. Have your friends been over at all?"

"Yeah. Frankie was here."

I thought that would make Mom feel better, but the lines between her eyes deepen. "How is he taking this? Was it okay?"

"Yeah," I lie. "It was great."

"You're a trouper, Josh. We're very proud of the way you're handling all this." I roll my eyes because I'm no trouper at all and besides, they wouldn't be very proud if they knew about the big secret hiding out in the shed. Mom smiles, kisses my forehead, and leaves. My book slips to the floor, and I lean back against the pillows. The air is stuffy. I go to the window and open it, letting the cold bite at my skin for a long time.

The night isn't silent. I've never noticed that before. There's not only the sound of an occasional car passing, but also the wind, touching the trees, the roof. There's the distant sound of a plane, the squeak of a bird, all sorts of tiny sounds, which have me thinking of Rachel, grinning as she holds the knife to her cheek, and of Max, in his cell, his eyes open in the darkness. In the end I crawl under the duvet with my clothes on. The light is on and my back is to the wall as I try to fall asleep with my eyes open.

I don't know how, but finally I sleep. In the morning my mother wakes me up, even though I don't need to go to school. "Honey, we're leaving," she says, half her attention on the PDA in her hand. "We've got an early meeting, and then we'll probably be gone all day. Will you be okay?"

"Sure."

"Don't answer the phone unless it's someone you know. Diane will look in on you around lunch, okay?"

I sit up fast. The duvet slips, and I remember I fell asleep in my clothes, but I manage to pull the duvet up to my chin before Mom notices. "Mom, I told you, I don't need a babysitter. I'm fine on my own. I don't want her around."

"Don't be like this, honey," Mom says. "She'll just be checking in on you, not babysitting you." She puts the PDA in her pocket and sits on the edge of my bed, brushes the hair from my forehead. "We feel terribly guilty leaving you alone every day, sweetie. At a time like this."

"I'll be fine. I'm fine. And I'm more fine on my own than with Dr. Die-Hard hounding me."

"Of course you'll be fine. And she'll check in on you just to be sure," Mom says firmly. "There's plenty of food in the fridge. Call us if there's a problem, or if you need anything. If you can't reach us, leave a message, then call Diane if it's urgent. Okay?"

"No freaking way am I calling her," I mutter, but it makes no difference. Mom leans over and kisses my cheek. Then she's gone, and a few seconds later Dad appears at my door and gives me more or less the same message. A few minutes later I hear the front door close.

I get dressed, sit down in Dad's office, and even though I

haven't been able to download those e-mailed assignments, I do homework. For an hour I can almost fool myself into believing everything's normal, that the worst thing in life is a looming math test.

I wonder if Rachel is still out there, or whether she's left. I can see the corner of the damn structure out the window, but there's no sign of her. Nothing except the curious absence of cats from the house, which Mom would have noticed by now if things were normal.

She must still be there.

But not for long. She doesn't have anything to eat out there except cat treats. She'll leave when she gets hungry.

At twelve o'clock on the dot, Dr. Ashe arrives. I knew to expect her, but when she appears in the doorway to the study, I nearly yelp. I should have guessed Mom had given her a key.

"Hello, Josh." She looks at me, and I almost feel her zooming in and out, like she did when I was flattened out on the laboratory slide. She's wearing jeans and a sweater, like a regular person, but in my head she's always wearing a lab coat. She always looks smaller in real life too, especially now that I'm taller than her. She smiles. "How are you doing?"

"Fine. Doing homework," I add, to show her just how fine I am.

She nods in approval but doesn't turn around and leave like I'd hoped. "Mathematics?" she asks, spotting the book on my desk. "Doing well in math, I'm sure? You have a natural aptitude for math . . . you both do . . ."

It's all I can do not to grind my teeth. Stupid aptitude tests. "I'm doing okay."

Seconds pass in awkward silence. Dr. Ashe has no kids, only a little girl who died long before I was born. I guess I should feel sorry for her, but she isn't too good at talking to kids, and I'm not too good at talking to scientists who've known me since I was a zygote.

"It's a terrible situation . . . ," Dr. Ashe murmurs at last, almost like she's talking to herself. She looks down, frowning. "I'm so sorry about this, Josh. So sorry."

I don't know what to say. So I don't say anything.

"Is there anything you need?" she asks at last. "If there's anything I can do. Are you okay for food? Has anyone been bothering you?"

"I'm okay. I wish I had my computer, but otherwise I'm fine."

"Your computer?"

"The cops took it," I say. "Looking for evidence."

"Oh." Dr. Ashe looks uncertain. "That's too bad. You need your computer to do your homework, of course."

I nod. Well, it's almost true. I do use it for homework, too.

Her face suddenly clears and she grins at me. "Aha—more importantly, you need a computer for games, right? Stuck at home day after day, and no computer games—that's got to be terrible!"

I feel chagrined. I don't want Dr. Ashe on my side. "Yeah," I mutter reluctantly. "That too."

"I can get you a laptop," she says, still smiling, like she's actually happy there's something she can do for me. "We've got some extras at the lab, for people to take on conferences and such. Would that help?"

"Yeah!" I try not to get my hopes up too high. I might not be able to play Genesis Alpha on a laptop, but just getting online would be fantastic. I could check out the message boards, maybe plan some missions, play some other games if that's all the laptop can handle. "That would be great."

"No problem. I'll bring it by tonight," she says. She reaches out, almost like she wants to pat my shoulder, but pulls back, turning the gesture into a halfhearted wave. I breathe easier when I hear the front door close behind her.

Mom and Dad call a couple of times that afternoon, but there's nothing new. Nothing they'll tell me, anyway, and I'm going crazy wondering what's going on. It must be even worse for Max, locked in a cell somewhere, but maybe they at least tell him something.

I watch the news, and Rachel Crosse is still missing. It's the top local story. The press is speculating about the possibility of Max not being the killer after all, that the real killer may have abducted Rachel. They also talk about that other possibility Dad mentioned, a copycat. They bring up the runaway theory, too, and a psychologist is consulted, spouting clichés about the stresses of a bereaved family, how Rachel might have run off to escape the oppressive presence of Karen's absence from the home, something weird like that.

I had hoped she was gone, but the cats have been absent

from the house all day, which probably means that Rachel is still out there. She must be hungry by now, even if she's snacking on cat treats.

I have to be certifiable, but when the six o'clock news says Rachel Crosse is still missing, I don't call the police. Instead I raid the fridge. I don't take too much, just enough to keep her from starving. Two pieces of fruit and some yogurt. There is a sink and running water out there, so she's not going to die of thirst, but I take her a can of soda too. When I step into the shed, I put the bag down by the door and don't say anything about it.

She's on the mattress, my MP3 player at her side, two blankets draped over her legs.

The cats are still all over her. They're purring. She's not. She snatches the headphones off and glares at me but doesn't say a word.

"Everybody's looking for you," I tell her. "Your family's worried you've been murdered. You have to go home."

"Really?"

"Yes." I sit down on the other end of the mattress. "You do."

She cranes her neck and looks toward the door. "I don't see anyone out there waiting for me. Did you call the police? Did you tell your parents?"

I shake my head, and Rachel looks smug. "Why not?" she asks as if she knows the answer.

I feel like shaking her until she stops smirking. I know I should tell Mom and Dad. I should call the police and let them know Rachel Crosse is not dead, she's right here, alive and okay—well, sort of okay.

But something about the way she mentioned Genesis Alpha yesterday gives me the creeps, and I need to find out what she meant. I don't want her to know though, because then she'd never tell me. So I can't ask. I have to wait for her to bring it up again.

"You didn't, because you can't," she jeers. "You know what I'll tell them." She stands up, and the cats jump off her lap and from her shoulders. She rolls up her sleeves and holds her arms out. "See?"

I take a step back and have to bite my lip to keep from gasping out loud. Her arms are black and blue, like someone has punched her again and again. There are also cuts, deep scratches with rough edges and torn skin.

"Who did this to you?" I breathe. Some of the cuts are old, some are fresh. It looks horrible. "Who hurt you like that?"

Rachel smiles. Her stretched mouth reminds me of the painted smile on a doll. A horror movie doll. "You did, of course. You grabbed me and you shook me and you punched me with your fists and you cut me with that knife. Remember?"

I stare at her arms, and then I discover something. Most of the cuts and bruises are on her left arm. I lean back in horror. She's even crazier than I thought. "You did this yourself."

Rachel calmly rolls down her sleeves. "If you tell anyone I'm here, I'll tell them you did it, and everybody will believe me."

I close my eyes. Why is she doing this?

But the thing is, I know the answer.

"Nobody will believe you," I say.

"They'll put you away," she says. "Lock you up in a cage, throw away the key, shave your head, and put the chair on sizzle. Just like they'll do to your brother."

"Stop it! Why don't you just go away and leave us the hell alone?"

"Why? So you can finish school and go to college and find a girlfriend and have a life, like my sister never will?"

She pushes Click and Cleo to the side with her foot and settles back down on the mattress, her back to the corner, her arms around her legs. "When they checked which embryo matched your brother, they did it by taking one cell away from you. Did you know that?" She looks at me with her eyes narrowed, but I don't answer. "I read about it," she continues. "They took one cell from you, out of just a few. Yanked one cell out of the bunch, ripped it off. That's a rather big chunk of you they cut off and threw away. I can't tell by looking at you, but there's a huge part of you missing."

"It doesn't work that way." She should know that. If she's read this much about the procedure, she knows the details. "The same DNA is in all the cells, and they're identical at that stage. Nothing is missing. The cells divide and make up for the loss."

"Oh, great, a biology lecture," she says, raising her eyebrows and making me feel like a total idiot. "But can you be *sure* nothing is missing?"

I don't have an answer to that. The truth is, I've often

wondered what happened to that part of me they took away. I know they didn't really take any of *me* away. Mom and Dad explained it all to me long ago, when they first told me I was the miracle that saved Max. Since then I've read about it myself, too.

But still, it's a strange thought that such a big part of me was cut away. I almost feel like I should be missing a hand or a foot, or something even more important.

"The whole is more than a sum of its parts," Rachel says. "Like, if they built a human being, cell by cell, there might still be something missing. Maybe your missing cell contained some essential part of your whole. Maybe your soul."

"Shut up."

"Was it worth it? Were *you* worth it? Do you think anyone's happy you saved your brother's life? Is anyone happy you exist?"

Rachel wants to hurt me. I let her. I'm angry somewhere deep inside, but piled on top of all that anger is tiredness and hopelessness and the knowledge that she's hurting worse than I am.

"Have you visited *him* at the jail?" she asks.

"You mean Max?" I wait for her to nod, forcing her to acknowledge his name. "No. Not yet."

"When did you last see him?"

"Maybe two months ago. He came home for a weekend."

"Did you touch him?"

It's creepy the way she won't say his name, and her questions are weird. But I can't help answering them.

"Sure. We shook hands when he said good-bye." Max also put his arm around me, both when we met and when he left, in a sort of hug, but I don't tell her that.

Rachel is suddenly there, standing in front of me. She's a bit shorter than I am, but not by much. She still smells of flowers. Flowers and cats. She takes my hand. Hers is cold.

"Like this?"

Her hand is smaller than Max's hand. Softer. "Yes."

"How did he hold it? Show me."

"Don't be stupid."

"Show me how."

I shake hands with her like I do with Max, palm against palm, my fingers around her hand. I feel like an idiot, and I don't know why I'm doing this. "Just a regular handshake."

"Just a regular handshake," she repeats. "Do you know how he killed my sister?"

"He didn't kill her."

She stares at me. Still holding my hand. I could yank it away if I wanted to, but she's holding very tightly. "Do you know how she died?"

"Of course I know."

"Did he tell you?"

"No! Everybody knows. It's been all over the news."

I try to pull away, but she tightens her grip, and I can't believe it, I can't believe she's stronger than I am, and I feel stuck, stuck to her, unable to get away, unable to escape, ever. "Let go!" I yell in sudden panic.

She lets go. Drops my hand so suddenly that I lurch back and almost fall. She wipes her own hand on her jeans, hard. "Just a regular handshake," she repeats with a sneer.

That evening, after my parents have called to say they won't be home for dinner, I'm eating microwaved lasagna and watching MTV when Dr. Ashe appears again.

"Hi there," she says. She smiles as she puts a large laptop case on the dining-room table and pats it with her hand. "Here you go. It's the most recent brand we have, and the biggest screen. I hope it's sufficient."

I stare greedily but remind myself not to get my hopes up. Laptops and Genesis Alpha aren't always a great match. "Cool. Thanks."

"It should help you pass the time," Dr. Ashe says. She puts a plastic bag with a familiar logo on top of the laptop case. "I got you some new video games, too. I don't know what kind you're into, but the guy at the store said someone your age would definitely appreciate these."

"Oh." I stare at the bag. "Thanks."

"No problem, Josh." She hesitates. "Are you doing okay?"

"Sure. I'm fine."

"Anything I can do?"

"No . . . the laptop is great. And the games. I really appreciate it."

"Okay." She puts her hands into her coat pockets and looks around. "Good. If there's anything I can do while your parents are busy, let me know. Anything. You have my number?"

"Yeah, sure. And, thanks. I mean, for the games and stuff."

"You're very welcome, Josh. And I mean it, if there's anything I can do . . ."

As soon as she's gone, I leave my dinner half eaten on the kitchen table and run upstairs with the laptop, booting it up as I go.

Not bad. I slide down in my chair, put the computer on my desk, and plug it in. It's a laptop, so not optimized for games, but it will do. I may have to lower the graphic settings so it doesn't stutter, but it should be good enough for Genesis Alpha.

I can't connect to the Internet. I rush down to Dad's study to check the router. It's gone too. I shout out in frustration, but then I remember the laptop has wireless, and I run back upstairs and fiddle with the settings until I connect with our neighbor's wireless router.

I start by downloading everything I need to enter Genesis Alpha. While it installs, I connect the laptop to my monitor, connect the keyboard, the mouse, then the speakers. After that I check my mail.

Hundreds of e-mails. I weed out the spam, but that still leaves lots of messages.

From Frankie, other friends, from kids at school, the homework from my teachers.

And a bunch from strangers. Most of the time the subject line is all I need to trash the messages. When they're not calling my brother a monster, they're calling me one for saving his life.

In the end I stop reading and trash everything that's not from someone I know.

Even those I'm not sure I want to keep. They're too interested, too excited, and it makes me angry and claustrophobic.

This isn't a TV reality show. It's real reality, and they have no idea. It's not fun. It's not exciting.

I log out of my mail without replying to anyone. I don't check anything else at all, not even to look up Rachel Crosse or check what's on the news about Max—or about me. I wait for Genesis Alpha to install, and then take a deep sigh of relief as the familiar opening screen greets me. I settle down in my spaceship and send a quick hi to my online friends.

I'm bombarded with messages and questions, both on my screen and in my ears. My friends from school are there, but everybody, even most of my foreign friends, seems to know what has happened.

"I'd rather not talk about it, guys," I tell them all. "I just want to play, okay?"

They don't give up easily, but when I turn off chat and block messages, they get the idea, and we just play. It's like being deaf. The sounds of the game come through, and being back on Genesis Alpha is like being home, but without my friends' chatter filling my ears and their messages cluttering my screen, I feel isolated. It's not the same.

But it's close enough.

"Josh?"

I jump at the sound of Mom's voice and turn away from

the screen. I'd forgotten everything, and time has passed. My stomach growls despite the lasagna dinner, and when I look at my watch, it's past midnight.

Mom looks at the laptop, frowning. "Where did that come from?"

"Dr. Ashe brought it. So I could do my homework."

She nods. "I'm sorry we were gone so long, honey. We couldn't help it."

"It's okay. I've been playing."

Mom nods. "Tomorrow," she says tiredly. "If you want to visit Max . . ."

Seven

He looks pretty much the same, only tired and sad. Even inside a small prison visiting room, even in an orange jumpsuit with handcuffs around his wrists. He even smiles the same when we greet him, and when I try to hug him, and he can't hug me back because of the handcuffs, I want to cry. The tight knot in my stomach loosens. It was stupid of me to doubt his innocence, even just for a split second now and then. This is Max, my brother. I've let everything get to me, I've allowed the media and a crazy girl in a shed to make me afraid of my own brother. Stupid and wrong.

"Hey, what's up?" he says. "It's good to see you."

"You too," I say. My voice sounds tiny in this room.

We sit down opposite him. There's a scarred green table between us. Max's hands are folded on top of it, the sleeves on his jumpsuit almost covering up the handcuffs.

His hands look just like normal hands, like my hands, but I can't help staring at them. I stare at Max a lot, while Mom and Dad chat with him about weird things, like the weather and TV shows or car racing. I don't say anything for a while, although Max keeps glancing at me, inviting me to say something. But I can't think of anything. I just sit there, looking at my brother, trying not to think about Rachel and the knife buried deep in my junk drawer.

There's a pause in the awkward conversation, and Max looks at me. He grins and I automatically grin back. "How are you doing?" he asks.

"I'm okay." It's not true, and I know Max knows that. I don't have to tell him.

"I'm sorry about all this," he says. "Mom and Dad tell me the press has been on your case about the designer thing. Your picture next to mine in the papers and everything."

"It's not that bad," I mutter. Max has enough to deal with. He doesn't need to worry about me. "I'm fine. Not your fault, anyway. They'll have to apologize when they release you and find the real killer."

"Judge and jury," Dad grumbles. "Why do we even bother with a judicial system when we've got both judge and jury in our living rooms around the clock?"

Max stares at me for a bit. "I can see why they put our pictures together," he says. "You're looking more and more like me every day. I guess that can't be easy right now."

I shake my head and blush because Max is reading my thoughts. I know how much I look like him, and if I went outside at all, it would probably be a problem. The short trip to the prison showed me that Mom and Dad were right to keep me home this week.

I'm going to grow my hair long. Max's hair is short. And

he's always neat. I've moved in the direction of scruffy. My jeans are torn, and I'm wearing an old denim jacket Dad owned ages ago. I shift in my seat, afraid Max has noticed, afraid he knows that I don't want to be like him anymore. It's not fair. I'm being disloyal to Max, over something that's not his fault.

"Are people giving you a hard time?" Max asks, frowning. I'm afraid to look at him, and my pulse has taken off, galloping without control. I don't know why. I'm not afraid of Max. I have no reason to be. He's my brother. He's innocent.

"You're right, Josh doesn't have it easy now," Dad says quietly. "I know it's worse for you, being locked up in here, but none of us has it easy these days."

"I guess you find out who your real friends are." Max's smile looks sad. "I wonder if I'll have any friends left when this is all over."

"Of course you will," Mom says. "For one, your roommate called yesterday. He sounded nice. He wanted to ask if there was anything he could do."

Max nods, and I think of Frankie. Maybe he's figured out a way to dig up the pictures of Max's room from the memory of his cell phone and has sold them to the highest bidder. How much would friendship be worth on eBay?

"Is school okay?" Max asks me. "Or are they on your case there too?"

"I haven't been to school," I say, and Max raises his eyebrows.

"We pulled him out of school for now," Dad says. "It's for the best while this blows over."

"Well, at least there's that," Max says. "I guess even with this there's a silver lining."

Mom clears her throat. "We have an appointment with your lawyer in five minutes, Max."

"My time isn't up," Max says, glancing up at the clock behind us. "I have ten more minutes. Maybe Josh can stay?"

"Are you okay with that, honey?" Mom asks me. "We'll be in a meeting room just across the hall. You can just pop on over when you're done."

"Sure," I say. I don't like it in here, but for Max I can stick it out for a few more minutes.

Mom turns to the guard standing behind us. "Our son's lawyer is waiting for us in the meeting room, so we have to go—is it okay if his brother stays until time's up?"

"That should be okay. Ten minutes," the guard says, moving closer, and Mom and Dad stand up to leave.

There's silence in the room after they're gone. I even hear the guard's breathing behind me, but I don't mind. My hands are clenched together and I stare at the tabletop, at the scars crisscrossing it. I wonder what made them.

"Hey, Josh?"

I look up. Force myself to look into his eyes, and smile. "Yeah?"

"You don't think I did it, do you?" Max asks. I shake my head hard, but I want to ask him, I desperately want to ask him if he did it, because even though I believe in him, I need him to tell me that of course he didn't. But I can't. I don't want him to doubt me, and if I ask, it's like I doubt him. I don't want him to think for a second that I'm not on his side.

Max lifts his shackled hands. "Someone sure thinks I did." He chuckles wearily. "So tell me. How are things in Genesis Alpha?"

"About the same," I say, almost dizzy at discussing Genesis Alpha in here. I remember Rachel's cryptic question.

Does your brother miss Genesis Alpha?

How did she know? Why does it matter?

"Did you finish the Toxic Mountain mission?"

"No, I couldn't by myself. Way too tough. I wouldn't even make it through the gate, let alone down to the engine room."

"You could get someone else to help you. You don't really need someone at my level. As long as you get someone close to your own level, if you're careful, you should be okay. If there are three of you, it'll be a piece of cake. Just make sure to bring lots of medical supplies and repair kits. Those guys can hit pretty hard, but it's worth it. Lots of good drops down there, and loads of mission points."

I shake my head. At least in this I can show my loyalty to Max. My faith in him. "No. I'd rather wait until . . . until you can play again."

"Might be a while," he says. "It's all circumstantial evidence, but Harris says it's enough to hold me for a couple of weeks."

"He'll get you out. He's a good lawyer, and they have no proof. They can't hold you in here forever just because you were in the wrong place at the wrong time."

Max leans back. The handcuffs scrape the top of the table,

and I guess I know now why the tabletop is so scarred. "Yeah. So what have you been doing with yourself?"

"Not much. The police—" I stop, dig my teeth into my lower lip because I shouldn't have brought up the police.

Max looks at me keenly. "The police what?"

"They took our computers," I mumble reluctantly. "So I couldn't do anything for a couple of days. Yesterday I got a laptop from Dr. Ashe, so I'm back online. But I've also got a ton of homework e-mailed from school, and Dad will probably make me do it all, and then some."

"Yeah, he will." Max grins. I can't believe we're talking about Genesis Alpha and homework over a green table boxed off by four concrete walls. I can't believe there are handcuffs around Max's wrists, and I can't believe there's a prison guard behind me, listening to every word we say. It's not such a bad feeling, though. It's kind of like being inside a computer game. The best kind of computer games, like Genesis Alpha, feel totally real at times. But most of the time when you're playing, there's a comfortable feeling of knowing it doesn't matter how much trouble you're in, it isn't *really* real—you can always reload or start from scratch. That's what this feels like. Like it can't be real.

"Dr. Die-Hard got you a laptop? She still hanging around?"

I nod glumly. "She pops up every day. Totally sucks."

"Hey, you're Diane's pet project, remember?" Max says. "She created you. She picked you out. So she likes to keep an eye on you. You'll probably never get rid of her."

"Yeah, well, she can go grow an ear on a mouse or something. I'm not in her lab anymore." I make a face. "But Mom and Dad ask her to check on me when they're gone all day."

Max smiles. "Yeah. I guess you really can't get away from her right now," he says.

"Pretty much. I'm stuck at home. People stare too much if I go outside." I don't tell him today was my first trip outside since all this happened. I don't tell him how a man outside the prison spat at us. Dad nearly attacked him—Mom had to drag him away.

Most of all, I don't tell him about Rachel.

"You do look a lot like me," he says again. "It's funny, isn't it, how alike we look? Maybe I took something more from you than just a few stem cells." He grins. "Ever thought of that? Maybe I got a lot more from you than we know."

He's sounding weird now, despite the light tone. But it's not really him. It's me. I'm imagining things because we're locked inside, because he has steel chains around his wrists, because we're in a cage meant for monsters. The atmosphere here makes me see monsters where there are none, even in my brother's face.

I'm getting claustrophobic and I clench my fists. I hate this place, but for my brother I have to tolerate it just a few minutes more. I can stand up anytime and leave if I want. Max can't. I owe it to him to stick it out. I force myself to sit still.

Max is still staring at me. "What do you think, Josh? Do you think I got the essence of your soul along with your stem cells?" He smiles, and I start to sweat, because the prison walls distort everything and his smile looks strange, making my chest tighten, making me forget that this is my brother, this is Max. Just Max. "After all," he adds, and his voice seems louder, coming at me from all directions in the eerie echo of this horrible room, "you were created just for me."

Max hates me.

The realization is stunning. Like someone hit me in the head and I'm left stumbling, wondering what happened and why, what is going on and who the hell I am.

My brother hates me.

Why?

Then the look is gone. Max is drumming his fingers on the table, and he looks tired and depressed, not scary at all.

"Just kidding," he says with a sigh. "That was a stupid thought. You think about the weirdest things when you're locked up twenty-four hours a day."

I imagined it.

I must have imagined it.

Sweat trickles down my back. My breathing seems loud, and I focus on the ticking of the clock behind me, yet I don't want to turn around to check it. I don't want to turn my back on Max. I don't dare turn my back on Max.

Why?

It's this place. It's not my brother, it's just this place. It's making me scared and paranoid and stupid.

Max is my brother. He doesn't hate me, and he's not a monster. I don't need to be afraid.

I tell myself all that, but I can't bring myself to turn around and check the clock.

"Time's up."

I shoot to my feet while the guard's words still echo in the room, and I'm ashamed of my relief. Did he notice?

Max looks annoyed. "Time isn't up," he says. "We've still got a few minutes."

"Time's up," the guard repeats, his face impassive.

"It's okay," I say quickly, but I feel guilty, like a traitor. Maybe the guard saw how scared I was all of a sudden. Maybe that's why the visit is over ahead of time.

"Hey, come see me again soon." Max smiles at me, one corner of his mouth higher than the other. It's an old smile, familiar, and as the door opens to freedom, the chains around my chest loosen enough to allow me to smile back at him without having to force my mouth to move.

This is my brother. This is Max.

I must have imagined it.

Eight

Brothers and sisters get half of their genetic material from each parent. And they each get half of the genes that each parent has. So brothers and sisters share on average 50 percent of their DNA. It can be more, it can be less, it all depends on which genes they get from their mother and father. Some siblings may share almost no genes, while others share almost all. Identical twins have identical genes, while fraternal twins are no more alike than any other siblings.

I do look a lot like Max. I don't know if the way I was selected as an embryo means that I'm more like Max than average. When they ran those genetic tests, they were looking for tissue types. Maybe matching tissue types also means that I'm like Max in other aspects, that we share more of our genes than average brothers do. Maybe we're more than brothers in that way too.

"Mom," I say in the car on the way home. It's a scary question, but it's bouncing around in my head and needs to get out.

"Yes, honey?"

"Hypothetical question . . ."

Mom turns around. "What?"

"If Max were guilty . . . would you forgive him?"

Mom's eyes widen, then narrow. "Josh, don't say that. Don't even think it. Your brother is not guilty."

"I know! I'm just saying. Hypothetically. If Max did something like that . . . or if I did something like that . . . , is it possible to forgive . . . ?"

Mom's eyes are blazing. "He's my son. That kind of a love is unconditional. It never dies, never fades. I will love him forever—I will love both of you forever—no matter what you do, no matter what happens."

I'm not sure about that. Everybody talks about unconditional love, but it's not really like that at all. Love is always conditional. There is a reason for everything, and there must also be a reason why you love someone. You can't get away with any horrible thing you can think of and still expect people to love you.

Mom sees the doubt in my eyes. "I guess you won't understand until you have children of your own," she says.

"So it's biological," I say. "People are wired to love their children no matter what. It's the way the species evolved. To keep us from extinction. So we'd take care of our children no matter what."

Mom hesitates. But she's a biologist. She can't deny this. She'd like to tell me love is something else, something magical and fantastic—not simply the product of serotonin and oxytocin and billions of years of evolution—but she can't. "Yes.

Of course it's biological. Everything we are can be traced to biology."

"So even if Max turned out to be a monster, or if I did, you'd still love us, because your brain chemistry tells you to."

Tears shimmer in Mom's eyes. She turns around without answering, and the rest of the drive home is silent.

When we get home, Mom says she has a headache and goes to lie down. I think the headache may be my fault. I sit with Dad in our kitchen for a while. He has a cup of coffee between his palms, and although I'd like to go upstairs and play Genesis Alpha, I stay, still thinking about my questions and Mom's answers.

Why do I love Max?

Because he's my brother. That's the simple answer. Because he's my big brother and I'm used to having him around and I like him and I love doing stuff with him. That can probably be linked to chemicals trekking around my brain. When we're with people we like, the chemicals in our brain give us a nice feeling. Do I like my brother because of brain chemistry, or does the brain chemistry happen because I like him? Or do I like him most of all because I saved him, because without me there wouldn't even be a Max, because without him there would be no me, because we're more than brothers?

"Things are looking better," Dad says. "They've been digging around for evidence, but of course they haven't found anything. Mr. Harris is optimistic. They probably won't be able to hold him much longer. We're hoping he'll be home before the end of the month."

"Home?"

"Yes. We'll talk about it when the time comes, but he'll probably stay here for the rest of the semester, start over next year. I think it would be best for him to find another college. Preferably out of state, so he'll get less attention. We can't allow the police's mistake to ruin his life."

I picture Max back in his old room, and the image flashes in my head, the way his eyes looked for that split second when I imagined he hated me.

After all, you were created just for me.

I drag myself to the shed because the litter boxes have to be cleaned, but I'm really not in the mood to deal with Rachel. So I ignore her. She's on the mattress, huddled under the blankets, Click sleeping in her arms, but I go straight to the litter boxes and get to work.

"Where were you today?" she asks at last. I straighten and look at her.

"What makes you think I was anywhere?"

"You weren't home."

"How do you know?"

She looks at me. "I know."

"You have until tomorrow," I tell her. "If you're still here tomorrow, I will call the police, and you can have all the fun you want trying to frame me. I'm not playing this game anymore."

"Where's my knife?"

"I don't know."

"I saw you pick it up from the ground. You have it. It's mine. Give it back."

"So you can keep cutting yourself? I don't think so."

Rachel smiles. She holds out her hand, and I shudder. She has driven a small nail through the flesh between her thumb and forefinger. She pulls it out while I watch, and blood leaks down to her wrist, soaks into the sleeve of her shirt, and then she keeps petting the cat like nothing happened. "I don't need a knife for that."

"They'll be letting Max go soon," I tell her. Angry. "They don't have enough evidence to hold him. Because he's innocent."

Rachel's whole body goes stiff. Her grasp on the cat tightens until he mews in annoyance and jumps free. "They can't let him go! He's guilty!"

I feel like screaming. "Don't you get it? How many times do I have to tell you? Max is innocent! There is no evidence! They'll never find any evidence because he didn't do it!"

"He did it. He did do it. I know he did. There is evidence."

"Oh, yeah? And just where is that evidence? In your crazy head?"

She looks up at me. Her eyes are green, but sometimes they seem more like blue. More like her sister's. "Genesis Alpha."

"What? What are you talking about?"

"Genesis Alpha. That's where he found Karen."

I stand still. Thoughts racing. Could she—? No. "That's impossible."

Rachel drags the rusty nail along the back of her hand. Tiny beads of blood ooze out. "No, it isn't. And there is evidence. Inside Genesis Alpha."

I sit down abruptly on a bag of cat litter. For a moment my legs are weak because she sounds so sure, because she sounds different now, sad, scared, less crazy. "How can there be evidence inside Genesis Alpha?"

"Mail. Chat logs," she says in a monotone.

"How do you know?"

"I know."

"How?

"His name is Rook. He's a half elf. A space warrior."

"Rook?" The relief is immense. I hide it by standing up and hauling the bag of kitty litter toward the litter boxes. "You're wrong. Max's character isn't called Rook. He's Alezander. He's an elf, not a half elf. I don't even know a Rook."

"I don't care. Your brother is also Rook. And Rook killed my sister."

"If Max is Rook, why haven't the cops found out?"

"They wouldn't bother to check out his games. To most people, games are just games. They don't realize games are reality too."

"You're wrong. They confiscated his computer. Even his old computer in his room at home. Even *my* computer. Their experts are going through all our computers, searching for evidence. They even interrogated me about all the aliases Max uses online. If there was something there, they'd have found it."

Rachel hesitates, then shakes her head. "Genesis Alpha

isn't saved to your computer," she says. "It's easy enough to cover your tracks."

I think about it, and technically she's right. To hide your character, you'd probably just have to delete one folder and make sure you overwrote it with something random, so it couldn't be dug up from the hard drive. It would be easy to do it automatically with a file shredder program.

It can be done that way. But that doesn't mean she's right about Max.

Her eyes focus on me. "Do you know your brother's password?"

I hesitate, but then I answer. "Yes."

Triumph flashes in her eyes. "If his password works for Rook, is that proof enough for you that Rook is his character?"

"Yeah," I answer, but then I think it over. It isn't conclusive proof. Someone could know Max's password. Someone could have set Max up. "No, wait," I add. "It isn't enough. Besides, if the password doesn't work, it won't prove anything either. You'd just say he used a different password."

"If the password works, there will be other proof," Rachel says. "From inside the game. And when they find proof that Rook did it, they'll get a warrant, they'll be able to trace Rook from Genesis Alpha to your brother's computer, even if they can't do it the other way around."

"You mean, to the killer's computer."

"Yes. The killer's computer."

"If you're so sure about this, why haven't you talked to the police?"

Rachel doesn't speak. She just keeps stabbing at the back of her hand with the rusty nail, and I'm really glad I didn't leave the knife out there.

"Why?" I repeat. "Why don't you just tell them? They could access the evidence easily. They'd just talk to the GMs and get all the information they need from the database."

Rachel looks up at me. Her jaw is clenched, but she's still pretending to smile. "I think this password will match. I want you to show me."

"I don't want to show you anything. Why should I? It won't match, but that won't prove anything to you, one way or the other."

"If the password doesn't match," she says, "I'll leave."

"Will you go home?"

"None of your business."

"Okay, fine," I say, shifting my weight. She'll leave. She'll finally leave, stop messing with my thoughts, stop making me doubt my brother with her crazy lies. "Okay. I'll go try it right now."

"You can't," Rachel says when my hand is on the doorknob. "Rook is only his nickname. It's a short form of his player name."

It makes sense. It's tricky to think up an original name in Genesis Alpha, because there are so many players. Like, Max wanted to be Alexander, but it was taken. So he put a *z* instead of *x*.

"Well? What is his full name?"

"I'm not telling you. You could destroy the evidence."

I sigh in exasperation. "Then what?"

"We have to do it together. Tomorrow. Will you be alone?"

I nod.

"I'll type in his name. You type in the password. We'll both see if the password works. We'll both see if evidence is there or not."

Nine

In the morning I'm out in the shed as soon as Mom and Dad have left. Rachel's asleep when I barge in, curled up on her side with the blankets over her. She sits up when I enter, blinks, runs a hand through her messy hair. The blanket moves, and Cleopatra emerges from under it, then collapses back down on the mattress, panting. The kittens in her belly must be getting heavy.

"Okay, let's do it," I say. "Mom and Dad are gone. Come on."

Rachel unties her ponytail, combs through her hair with her fingers, then reties it. I gaze at the blond strands that escape the ponytail and tickle her neck instead. Her hair looks soft and silky even though she's been here for days. She must be washing it in the sink, with the old bar of soap and the trickle of icy water.

"Come where?" she asks, and I feel my face warm when she looks up at me and smirks, as if she knows what I'm thinking.

"To the computer. To check on that Rook guy, remember?"

I shift my weight from one foot to the other. "Come on!" I can't wait to get this over with. I want her gone.

"In the house? Your house? *His* house?"

"Where else?"

"A netcafé. There's one in the mall. Half an hour on the bus."

"Come on, that's just stupid. Both our faces are on the news every day. Yours is probably on posters too. We'll be recognized." I bite my tongue. Maybe I should have gone along with her way. Rachel would be seen, and someone would tell the police and take her home.

Of course, she'd also be seen with me.

Not a good idea.

She pulls the blanket over her shoulders. She's shivering. "We could cover our hair with baseball caps. Wear sunglasses."

"Yeah, like that would work."

"But . . ." Rachel sounds small. She rubs her eyes but can't seem to think of anything to say.

"Come on," I repeat. "If you want to do this, we'll have to do it now. Unless you're stalling. Unless you've just been bluffing."

She stands up and glares at me, which feels a lot better than her sounding all small and fragile, and when I turn around and leave the shed, she follows me.

It's weird to have Rachel in our house. She's quiet as she follows me through the back door and up the stairs. She doesn't ask about Max's room, but she looks at the door with the KEEP OUT sign, like she knows that's the one. When we get to my room, I'm a bit embarrassed about the mess. Girls care about stuff like that much more than guys do. But she doesn't seem to notice.

We sit down at the desk. Rachel sits to the left, closer to the door. I sit to the right. There's a lot of space between us.

My keyboard is a bit greasy from yesterday. I was eating potato chips last night while I was playing. Max would hate that. Max has a thing about dirty keyboards. He doesn't like using other people's computers, and he doesn't like it when other people use his. When he was still at home, I'd borrow his computer sometimes, and he always found out, no matter how careful I was to leave everything exactly the way it was.

Rachel is biting her fingernails, but at least she's not clawing at her skin. She's not even looking at the screen. I log on to Genesis Alpha, see the familiar entry screen, delete my username, which appears automatically, then push the keyboard her way. "Okay. Type in the username."

She does. With one ragged fingertip.

Rook2King.

She leans back and looks at me, her eyebrows low, her face pale, but she's not shivering anymore.

I put my hands on the keyboard, trace the raised bumps on the F and J keys with my fingertips. I have a choice. I can make up a phony password and get rid of Rachel. I know the username now. I can always try it later, when I'm alone, when Rachel isn't watching.

"Go on!" Rachel growls.

The decision is in my fingers, not my head. I type it in. Max's password, the one I've used with his permission so many times: MyPAzw0rd.

I hold my breath, waiting for the familiar message when I mistype my own password: "Wrong password. Try again?"

Yes!

I lean back, tension draining from my body. I can almost feel it rush away through my pores. I don't know why I was even worried, and I hate myself again, I hate that tiny part of me that's never sure about anything, not even Max's innocence. "See? Not him."

"He used a different password," Rachel says, her voice thin with disappointment. "Or maybe you're the one bluffing. Maybe you didn't input his real password. You didn't, did you? You've covering up for him."

"I'll try his other passwords," I snarl at her, dizzy with relief, but also angry because this isn't proof enough for her, nothing will ever be proof enough for her, and nothing will ever convince her Max is innocent.

Max always uses the same basic password, but some programs require you to change it every now and then, and both of us use the same technique, changing the numeral. I start typing, rush through the sequence, feeling stupid because this won't convince her either, nothing will convince her.

MyPAzw1rd

MyPAzw2rd

MyPAzw3rd

My stomach cramps when on the third try the screen

explodes into a familiar kaleidoscope of colors. I stop breathing in shock.

This can't be.

I stare at the screen, Rachel silent by my side, no victory shout as I'd have expected. We watch the fractal forms squirm around the screen, and it feels normal, because I do this every day. The colors will settle, subtly shift until they form an image, the player's starting location, his home. Some players have a castle or a dungeon or a tower. Others have a moon base or an asteroid or a comet. It can be whatever they want. Max's character, Alezander, has an underwater cave. It's dark, but still colorful, with lots of life in it, fish and frogs and insects. My home is a laboratory. No people, no animals. Just equipment and chemicals. I'm a wizard. Alezander is a warrior.

The kaleidoscope settles. It's a mountaintop. A desolate place. There's a small hut, and stone steps leading down the mountain. A spaceship sits on a platform. It's a Nasarus battle cruiser, my favorite ship. I have one just like it, only differently configured.

Outside the hut sits an open wooden chest. I flip through the inventory. Many fancy items, high-level, expensive. Some of them I've never seen before, but others I recognize. A Bloodstone axe, superspeed boots, a Tracker machine gun. Some of Max's favorite things.

But that doesn't prove anything. There is a limited number of items in the game. Many players share the same favorite objects.

Rachel is still by my side, but she's so motionless and quiet I almost stop noticing her. I stare at the screen, fingers moving automatically on the keyboard and the mouse. I'm Rook. I'm seeing the world with his eyes, playing his game. He's a high-level character with a long game life, he's even stronger than Alezander. A fighter with good stats, good equipment, plenty of gold, the amazing spaceship with expensive extras.

"Check his mail," Rachel says. She has moved on to her thumb, her teeth ripping at the skin around the nail.

I feel like a burglar. Like I'm inside someone's house without permission, looking at their personal things, rifling through their secrets. The first few minutes I feel funny moving Rook around like he's my own avatar, but then it becomes natural. I walk Rook around outside his hut, look through his treasure chest, dress him in the best pieces of armor.

"Check his mail," Rachel repeats, her voice indistinct with her teeth sinking into her thumb.

I take my time about it. I check Rook's stats more closely. I look at the details of his quests, the missions he has completed.

Rook is Max's character. I'm sure of it now. I recognize so many of Max's favorite game objects, but worse than that, Rook and Alezander even have the same tattoo on their chests, the same aliases and key combinations. That can't be a coincidence.

It doesn't prove anything. Max is allowed to have as many characters as he wants. That doesn't make him a killer.

My mouth is dry, but I still stall. I check his buddy list. Nobody I know, but a lot of girl names. That's different. Alezander and I mostly have guy friends on Genesis Alpha.

Finally, in my own good time, I enter the hut. It's empty. There's nothing there except the mailbox. It's sitting on the floor, revolving, which means there is unread mail. I walk to the mailbox and open it. I scroll through some of the recent letters, just checking the name of the sender and the date. There are a few unread messages. Nothing important there, just people—girls—asking where he is because they haven't seen him recently.

There's also a lot of old mail, from many different people. It goes back almost a year, from before I started playing Genesis Alpha.

I stop scrolling and open one of the old messages. Another one. And a third one. Beside me, Rachel reads too. I hear her breathing. Deep, labored, like she's running uphill.

The mouse feels cold under my fingers and goose bumps spread all over my body as I slowly make my way through his mailbox.

Rook knows so many girls. Or at least players who claimed they were girls. In Genesis Alpha, that doesn't always mean they really are.

I pick one girl's name and read their mail exchange, starting from the earliest posts. I'm a fast reader, but Rachel seems equally quick, because she never tells me to slow down. But when I glance to the side, I see she's not reading at all. She's staring at the screen, but her eyes aren't following the text. She's biting at her index finger now, her teeth ripping at the skin and the nail, leaving the ragged edges she uses to scratch her arms.

It's just mail. Just like regular e-mails you'd exchange with a girl. They're talking about the game, about college, about music and TV shows. I stop, shut the mailbox, and lean back. "There's nothing there."

"You're not done," Rachel says. She leans over, clicks the mouse, opens the mailbox again. Then she settles back, her teeth gnawing at her finger again, staring at the screen in that blind way of hers.

"It's private. And it's not proof. It's just a guy and a girl, talking. It's innocent."

"It's not innocent," Rachel says. "And it's not private. Not anymore."

I force myself to keep reading, and with each letter I feel colder and colder. It's not innocent. It can't be innocent. Rook is sneaky. Patient. Not everybody he chats with is careful, but he isn't interested in girls who immediately tell him their names. He's interested in the ones who are cautious, the ones who resist his initial attempts to get information out of them. He chats with the girls over weeks, months. Only mails are here, no chat logs, so I only see a part of the picture. It's enough. Rook drags out of them one tiny detail after another, so slow and subtle that they don't even notice how much they're giving away.

It looks bad. It looks very bad.

It looks like Genesis Alpha was where Rook searched for a victim.

Where *Max* searched for a victim.

Rook puts it all together in a memo, titled with each girl's character name. He adds details as he discovers them. Their real name. The name of their college. The name of their town, friends' names, siblings' names, parents' occupations. Hobbies, interests, plans for the future. Several memos are marked with a gold star. They have a name and an address at top; the other memos don't. So I think a gold star means he knows enough about them to track them down.

Maybe he already has.

I look at the first few gold-starred memos, but then I stop. I'm afraid I'll recognize one of the names.

"Which one is your sister?" I ask.

"None of them," Rachel replies.

For a second I'm relieved. But then I see the look on Rachel's face. "What do you mean?"

Rachel smiles. It's a bizarre image—her sharp teeth are still mauling her index finger. "It wasn't Karen he met on Genesis Alpha."

"What?"

She smiles wider, her mouth stretching into her cheeks like a rubber mask. "It was me."

Ten

Lehcar.

The fifth gold-starred memo.

I open it and see Karen's name.

Rachel's chair scrapes on the carpet. I hear her footsteps thud on the stairs. She's gone. I wait a few minutes, my eyes frozen to the memo on my screen, but she doesn't return.

I don't know what to do. I don't know what to think, I can't think with the tornado swirling in my head, the horrible sick feeling in my stomach. This doesn't feel real, it feels like a bad dream, like being stuck inside a nightmare with no way out. I'm looking at proof. I'm looking at evidence that Max is a murderer.

But it can't be. It can't be Max. It can't be for real. There must be an explanation, it must be a mistake.

I access his mailbox again and continue reading his mail. Rachel's letters this time. I know she doesn't want me to. I'm not even sure I want to. But I read every last word, every one of their mails, and the room feels colder and colder.

I'm shivering by the time I leave the hut and put Rook's

stuff back in the chest, getting ready to quit the game. I hesitate before clicking quit.

I should save this.

I don't want it on Dr. Ashe's computer though. I rummage in my bottom drawer until I find Rachel's pocketknife. I locate the flash drive on it, flip it open, and connect it to the computer. The knife looks creepy sticking out of the laptop, buried in its side, so I hurry, export Rook's character and his mailbox to the memory key, unplug it, and push the knife deep into my pocket.

I log off, erase the player file so there's no trace of Rook on the laptop. Then I log in as myself, close the chat channel, and find myself a difficult solo mission. Eventually I stop shivering.

When lunch has passed and nobody shows up, not my parents, not even Dr. Ashe, I check the shed, not really expecting Rachel to be there. But she's there. Alone. No cats.

I sit at the other end of the mattress, back against the wall, my arms around my knees. After a while I notice we're breathing in sync.

"Did you read it all?" Rachel asks at last.

"Yes."

"You see. He did it."

"Yes," I whisper, saying aloud what's been growing in my head since I first saw Rook. "He did it."

Rachel makes an odd sound. Her hands cover her face, her hood covers her hair. She's a puddle of darkness, and I wish my dad were here. Dad always knows what to say. Most of the time it's very annoying, but he'd be useful now.

"He guessed." Rachel's voice drifts from the black heap. "Lehcar. It was a stupid name for me to pick, wasn't it? He guessed my name was Rachel. Mom's a freak about Internet safety. I get endless lectures about keeping safe. So I panicked. I said the first thing that popped into my head. I told him, no, it wasn't Rachel, it was Karen." She moans. "Stupid."

"You told him a hell of a lot more," I blurt out. It was all there, in the memo. Karen's college. Her major. Her sorority. All sorts of details. More than enough to track her down. Some of it I found in their e-mail exchanges. But most of it must have come from their chats.

I see the glint of her eyes as she raises her head. "Yes. I told him everything. Everything he needed to know."

Sneaky. Patient. One little fact this week. Another one the next month. A clue, a hint, accidental slips here and there. One detail at a time, until he had enough pieces of the puzzle to put his horrible picture together.

"Rook told me about you."

"What?"

"Rook talked about you. He thought you were cool for a little brother. He liked your computer graphics stuff. You make spaceships and robots."

I nod.

"He said you played Genesis Alpha together. I asked him about your game name, so I could say hi, but he wouldn't tell me."

My head spins. Rachel has talked about Max as something

subhuman. But she talks about Rook with familiarity. I see Rook as the killer, Max as my brother, a real person. For her it's the other way around.

"He said his little brother was about the same age as my little sister. Which is me. I was my little sister." She mutters something under her breath. I think she's saying "stupid" again.

"What else did he say about me?"

"Not a lot. Not that you were a designer baby or anything. He was careful. I wasn't the only one, was I? He had a whole list of girls. Maybe Karen wasn't the only one he killed. Or maybe he was just getting started, and she was the first."

Goose bumps start crawling around my body again. "I don't know."

"I met Rook three months before he killed Karen. I talked to him almost every day for three months, and I didn't realize what he was. He was normal. I didn't know. He seemed so normal. Like you. It's easy, isn't it? Easy to pretend to be normal. But then I got suspicious. Of little things. Like, I told Rook I didn't have a boyfriend. A little while later, he asked again. If I was sure I didn't have a boyfriend. He sounded jealous. When Karen came home for a weekend a bit later, I found out she had a new boyfriend. There were other things, small things. He mentioned something he wasn't supposed to know. Like, I told him I hated cigarettes, couldn't stand the smell. And he acted surprised. Like he didn't believe me. I'd forgotten Karen smoked. Little things like that. So I got nervous. Then I got paranoid enough to quit the game." She digs the toe of her sneaker into the floorboards. "I spent almost a year building up my character. Lehcar. She was a scholar, seventeenth level. I had to start from the beginning again, all because of Rook."

"You still play?"

"No. I did. For ten more days. Until Karen died. I was only up to third level with my new character."

"But how could you be sure Rook was the one who killed her?"

"I wasn't. I didn't have proof. Not until you showed me."

"I don't understand. If you suspected him . . . if you knew he was watching Karen in real life . . . if you suspected he was stalking her . . . if you were so nervous you quit the game . . . why didn't you tell someone? Why didn't you warn her?"

Cleopatra emerges from the tunnel. She rubs against my legs on her way to Rachel. Rachel curls her body around the cat, her knees up, her head down, her hood drawn down over her face, turning herself into a shadow, fading into the wall.

I shut up. And I understand why she's making herself bleed.

"Where do you think evil comes from?" Rachel asks much later, when the shadows have gotten longer and Cleo has vanished inside, to wait with the others for dinner to appear. She stretches, raises her arms so her hands and wrists shine white above her head, but her face is shadowed by the hood on her sweater.

"I don't know."

"Where is it stored? In our brain? Are there evil brain cells? Evil synapses? Evil neurotransmitters? Evil brainwaves? Where exactly is it?"

She's asking the kind of questions I like to ask my parents, but I don't think all the research in the world can answer these questions. "I don't know."

"Maybe there are evil stem cells."

I yank my head up in surprise. I can't see her face, but I can imagine a thrill of joy in her eyes at getting a reaction out of me.

"That could be where evil comes from," she continues. "Maybe Max is really innocent. Maybe he couldn't help it, he got evil from your cells. Maybe it spread all over him from you."

"If evil is anywhere, it's in our brain. The human part of our brain."

"What do you mean, the human part?"

I flounder, wishing Mom and Dad were here to whisper the correct answer in my ear. "It's . . . our mind. Whatever makes us different from the animals. The ability to . . . think like that. I guess."

Rachel tilts her head to the side in that way I've come to dread. "So, does that mean evil comes with intelligence? Is evil smart?"

"I don't know. But evil is human."

"Can you create evil? When you raise a kid, can you make him evil even if he's born good?"

"Maybe. I guess. Maybe the kid wouldn't know the difference between good and evil if nobody taught him. Or if they taught him wrong."

"What did your parents teach you and Rook?"

I don't answer.

"Mom and Dad want Karen's killer dead. They want to see your brother die. Is that evil?"

I know that when a murderer gets the death penalty, families of the victims have the right to watch them die. I wonder how it works. Would they sit in the same room as my mom and dad while they watched Max die?

Sometimes I don't like being human at all.

"Is it?" Rachel demands.

"I don't know."

"Maybe you should die too," Rachel said. "You deserve it. My sister wouldn't be dead if it weren't for you."

My anger is a molten flash, it burns up through my lungs and explodes through my vocal cords. "What about what *you* did?" I shout at her. "You set her up. You gave her to Max. And you never warned her. She's dead because of *you!*"

Rachel smiles. It's the rubber mask smile, and I shut my mouth, bend my head and hit my forehead against my knees, hard. Stupid. Stupid, stupid, stupid. This is what she wanted, and I walked right into it. She taunted me on purpose so I would slash back. She used me, just like she uses a rusty nail or a wood sliver or the Swiss Army knife, and I let her.

"It can be like a game," Max once told me, a long time ago when I asked why he kept teasing his high school girlfriend, making her run away in tears. "To say different things and do different things and watch the way people react. I can call

Nora right this minute, and if I say the right thing, she'll come rushing back here. But people are pretty predictable, you know. It gets boring after a while."

Late that night Dad's sitting at his desk, a red pen in his hand, a pile of papers to his left and a bigger one to his right.

I love my dad's office. When I was little, I'd sometimes sneak downstairs after I was supposed to be asleep, while Dad was up late, preparing a lecture or grading papers. He'd scowl when he saw me in the doorway, but then he'd push away the paperwork and hold out his arms. I'd crawl into his lap and put my arms around his neck and lean my head against his shoulder. And he'd tell me stories. Not fairy tales or fantasies, but real stories. Stories I couldn't read in any children's book. He told me about ancient kingdoms where brothers married their sisters, about autistic children who can calculate impossibly high prime numbers but don't know what a smile means, about how experiments and history show that most people will hurt others if someone in a white coat or a uniform tells them to.

But he never told me a story about a brother betraying a brother.

For days I've been afraid that my brother is guilty. But *knowing* he's guilty changes everything.

I have no choice. There is proof.

Without proof, they might let him out. And he might do it again. Rook might return to Genesis Alpha, he might go back to his hut, sit on the floor and sift through his memos, and maybe hunt down another girl.

It's up to me to turn him in.

But if I tell, and Max is sentenced to death, then I will have killed my brother.

I walk to Dad's desk. Trail my hand on its edge and remember when the edge of the table was the height of my shoulder instead of my hip.

"Josh." Dad takes off his glasses and rubs his eyes tiredly. "You're still up."

I look down at his hands resting on the table. Once, both my hands could vanish inside one of his, but now our hands are the same size. For a moment I wish he'd grow bigger. That everything in this room except me would grow bigger, so I could crawl into Dad's arms and be safe there like I could when I was little.

Instead I lean against the wall, slide down until I'm sitting on the floor.

"What's wrong?" Dad asks.

"Dad . . . ," I say, and he leans closer because my voice is so low. "If you knew . . ."

"What?" Dad says.

"If you knew . . ." There's a lump in my throat. It stops the words.

"If I knew what?"

"If you knew Max was guilty . . . if you knew there was evidence . . ."

Dad's eyes widen. "What? It's not poss—" He pauses. I see his throat move as he swallows. He shakes his head slowly. "Josh?" he whispers.

It hurts, like talking with a sore throat, and my face is burning up, but I force the last words out. "What would you do?"

Dad's still staring at me. Then he stands up. He holds out a hand, and when I take it, he pulls me to my feet. He cups my face in his hands and brushes his thumbs over my cheekbones. Tears. I'm crying. Dad holds me tight, and I bury my face in his shoulder just like when I was little, squeeze my eyes shut and bite the inside of my cheeks to keep from sobbing like a baby. It feels weird when he hugs me, because I'm as big as he is now, and although I'm used to it, now it feels like I should be little.

Then Dad grabs me by the shoulders, shakes me gently. I open my eyes. His face is pale, his eyes damp. He looks almost as afraid as I feel. If he doesn't ask, I won't say anything more.

But Dad is braver than I am.

"Tell me," he says.

Eleven

I tell Dad about Rook. I tell him about the passwords, the fourth password in the sequence working, and I tell him about the evidence inside the game.

I don't tell him about Rachel.

I mean to. I'm just not sure how.

Dad, the girl on the news, the sister, the one who's missing . . .

Dad . . . you know, Karen Crosse? Well, her sister . . .

Dad, I've been hiding a fugitive crazy girl out in the shed. . . .

No. None of it quite works. And maybe I don't have to say anything about Rachel. Maybe now that we have Rook's computer records, she'll go home, leave me alone.

"I'll handle it," Dad says a long while later, after we've accessed Genesis Alpha together. He has asked a lot of questions, and the answers have tumbled out of my mouth, and then there was an eternal silence while Dad scrolled through the letters, and as he read more and more, as he saw the list of gold-starred memos, his breathing sped up like he was running. His forehead is damp, his eyes red because he keeps rubbing them. "Leave this to me. You don't have to get involved, Josh."

He means, Max doesn't have to know I turned him in.

Mom doesn't have to know I turned Max in.

"Are you going to the police?"

"Don't worry," Dad says quietly. "I'll deal with it."

"Max did it?" Although I mean it to be a statement, it sounds like a question. A question I want him to deny. I want him to figure out some logical explanation for the evidence not being what it seems.

"How do I log out of this game?" Dad asks.

I show him. He makes a note of Rook's username and password. Taps his pen against the pad for a long time. He has made a lot of notes. I don't look at them.

"What are you going to do?" I ask again, because he didn't answer and suddenly I'm afraid he won't take this to the police. Afraid Max will come home. Afraid Rook will return.

"I'm going to talk to Max," he says at last. "He deserves a chance to explain this."

But what if he asks Dad not to tell? Will Dad be able to refuse?

"What about Mom?"

There's a long pause. The taps of the pen against paper have formed a tornado of tiny dots under Max's password. "I'll wait a bit to tell her," Dad says. "I mean, he was obviously stalking the girls, but maybe . . ." He breaks off. "Your mother is very fragile right now. I'll talk to Max first."

I dream that night. I dream I'm in the shed with Rachel. There's a snowstorm outside, the small windows white with snow and the wind shrieking through the cracks in the walls. Between us is a makeshift table, made out of three old car tires piled on top of each other and a round wooden board on top. On the table is a candle. It flickers in the draft, and our shadows are spastic on the walls. It's cold. Our breaths are foggy, our hands white. Somewhere, a clock ticks. We're waiting for Max to die. We wait and the ticking gets louder, until at last, it stops. Just stops. I hold my breath, and I know Max is dying. Max is dying, and I can't breathe, yet I can't stop breathing . . .

My parents are out when I wake up. Mom has left a note on the kitchen table with a P.S. in Dad's handwriting: "Eat breakfast!" Some things never change. I make a face at the note but go get my cereal. Apparently brainwashing does work.

I go out to the shed, but there's nobody hiding in the shadows. Three of the cats are there, looking for her. Cleopatra lies on the mattress where Rachel used to be, her nose quivering.

It's over. She's gone.

I go online for a while, but it's hard to concentrate. I keep thinking about Rook, keep seeing him when it's just someone in a Nasarus battle cruiser or the flash of someone's Bloodstone axe.

The cats wander in and out of my room like they used to before an automatic treat dispenser took up permanent residence out in the shed. But a few hours later they've all disappeared. When not even the sound of the dry cat food pouring into their bowls brings them running, I pull on a sweater and my boots and run out to the shed. It was too good to be true.

There's a new smell there. Rachel has lit a cigarette. It dangles from her mouth. And there's a bag on the mattress next to her. Sandwiches and juice cartons.

Tuna cans.

"I thought you were gone," I say.

"I was. I came back."

"Where did you go?"

She blows a smoke ring. "I needed some groceries."

"Groceries."

"Yep."

"Didn't anyone see you leave the yard?"

"I went through the forest." She gestures in the direction of the trees stretching into our backyard. "Nobody saw me."

"Didn't anyone recognize you?"

She puts a baseball cap on her head, pulls it down over her eyes. "No. Guess I'm not as famous as you think I am."

I don't know what to say.

"You said you hated cigarettes," I say at last.

"I do. I started smoking the week after Karen died." Rachel blows more smoke rings and looks at me like I'm supposed to be impressed. "She came home a lot. At least once a month for a weekend. She wasn't supposed to smoke at home, but she did, in her room." She crinkles her nose. "You could smell it just by walking past her room, even with the door closed. Not just when she was home, but all the time."

She inhales. Holds her breath for a moment, then exhales a plume of smoke, grimacing, like it tastes bad. I step back. "After she died, the stink went away. It happened so quickly. It was weird, you know. Sometimes she wouldn't come home for a whole month, but the smell was still there, no matter how much air freshener Mom sprayed or how often she opened the window. But after Karen was gone, the smell disappeared so quickly. So I go in there, once in a while, and smoke a cigarette to bring the smell back. My parents still go in there, you know. Just stand there and breathe. So I spray her perfume around and I smoke her cigarettes." She looks around. "Where are the cats? They were here a minute ago."

"They probably left when you lit up. They hate cigarette smoke."

Rachel stubs out the cigarette. Waves her hand in the air to disperse the smoke. "I went to the cemetery too." She looks at me. "To Karen's grave."

I shuffle my feet, not sure what to say.

"My parents go all the time. Like every week. Just to stand there. It doesn't even have a headstone yet. There's just a white cross with her name. And flowers. They take her flowers every week. They cry. And they talk. Sometimes they even talk to Karen, like she's there, listening to them. And then they want to hug me, because I'm all they have left. I hate it. I hate everything about it. So I refuse to go there, and they think I'm a bad sister, but why should I, anyway? It's not like she's there. There's nothing in the ground but a rotting body inside a coffin. Karen's not there. She's not anywhere."

"Why did you go there, then?"

"I had to." She slips the cigarette stub into her jacket pocket. "I needed to bury a queen in her grave."

"A queen?"

"A white queen."

"You mean a chess queen?"

"The queen always beats the rook," she says. "Always. A queen beats anything, one on one. And the king—well, the king is just a joke. Do the police know yet?"

"Yes," I say, because it's simplest, easiest, and because I don't know what Rachel would do if I told the truth—that I have no idea what Dad will do.

She nods.

"You have to go back home. You need to go home now."

She shakes her head. "No."

"Don't be stupid. You can't stay here forever."

"I can't," she says. "I can't go home. Don't you understand?"

"Unless your parents are beating you or something, no, I don't understand. They're freaking out. They're afraid they've lost you too. Everybody has pretty much written you off already, but they're still hoping you'll be found alive."

She stares at me and doesn't blink. "That's the point. Don't you see?"

"No. I don't see."

"When they found Karen, there was no hope anymore."

Twelve

By the time my parents are home, I'm in Dad's study, half-heartedly doing a biology assignment.

They always seek me out to say hello when they get in. But not this time. After a while I go search for them. They're in the kitchen. And there's total silence. Mom's standing by the window. It looks like she's staring out, but the curtains are closed, so she's just staring at the yellow-and-orange pattern. Dad's sitting down. His hand is clenched around his mug, but there's nothing in it.

I hesitate, wonder if I can sneak away, but Dad notices me. He waves me closer with a tired gesture. Mom doesn't budge.

"What's wrong?" I whisper, without meaning to.

Dad clears his throat. He's pale. Looking more tired than he ever has during this entire mess. "Max confessed," he says.

By the window there's a sharp movement. Then stillness again. Dad rubs his eyes. "Harris discussed new evidence with him. His options. And he confessed to the murder."

"False confessions," Mom says in a monotone. "The pressure, the stress and confusion of being in prison. Happens all the time. Stress-induced hallucinations . . . they may even start believing they committed the crime they're accused of . . ."

Dad's sigh is almost inaudible. "Laura. Please."

Mom sways, ever so slightly, like she can't quite hold her balance.

"He knows things he shouldn't," Dad says quietly. "About . . . about what was done to the girl. Information the police had been keeping secret." He lets out a shuddering sigh. "I don't want to believe it either. I can't believe it. I can't believe Max did this. But we don't have a choice anymore."

"Don't give up on him, Jack," Mom pleads. "There has to be an explanation. Maybe he's covering up for someone. Maybe it's some kind of an honor code . . . maybe someone told him about it, and he got confused and horrified . . . and then the police grabbed him and put him in jail, and now he thinks he did it. . . ."

I'm numb with disbelief, even though I was the one who found the evidence. Even though I've known since yesterday that Rook was guilty.

I've been thinking about Rook all day. Rook in his armor, with his axe. Rook, stalking the galaxy in search of prey. Rook, a ruthless killer.

Rook. Not Max.

But Max confessed. Because Max is Rook. They're the same. Not separate.

Relief mingles with the sadness and disbelief and fear tingling all over my body. Max has confessed. It can't get any worse than this. It will be over now.

Then I look at my parents, and I know it will never be over.

"He can't have done it," Mom continues. "We just have to find out why he thinks he did . . . why he says he did . . ."

Dad is silent. Mom's breathing is loud. Her arms are folded around her body, and she stares at the closed curtains. Her shoulders are so tight, her neck almost disappears. Slowly they lower.

"What could we have done?" she whispers. "How did we . . . ? How could we have made a monster?" She crosses the floor quickly, reaches up on a shelf, yanks at the cookbooks. They plummet down until every title is lying in a heap on the floor. "What's the recipe for a monster, Jack?" she shouts. "Did we include all the ingredients? Because, you see, I don't remember molesting Max. I don't remember abusing him. I don't remember neglecting him. I don't remember making him feel worthless. What was it? What did we do?"

Dad reaches out toward Mom, but she shoves him away. "How?" she screams. "How? And what does this mean for Josh? What will this do to Josh?"

Dad looks at me. *Don't worry*, his eyes say, but this time I'm not sure I can believe him. *Go to your room*, a sharp twist of his head says, but I ignore it. "Laura . . ."

"They'll kill him, you know," Mom says. "If he's a . . . murderer." She chokes on that phrase. "They'll execute him. They'll kill my baby."

"No, Laura. He confessed. He's cooperating with the authorities. It counts in his favor."

"Then what? Will we visit him once a week until we die from old age? Will we look at him through a glass wall and know we caused the death of an innocent girl by bringing him into the world? And what about Josh?"

"What about me?"

Mom doesn't hear me. "When Max was sick, I'd have done anything to make him better. Anything. If someone had offered me a deal, his life in exchange for the life of an unknown girl . . ." Mom hesitates. "Maybe that's what happened. Maybe I did make a pact with the devil. My son's soul and the life of this girl in exchange for the cure."

"Laura!" Dad says. He tries to hug her, but she pulls away. "Calm down. You're being hysterical."

Mom slides down onto a chair. Stares at me, like I'm a stranger. "From the day you were born, Josh, everything was perfect. *You* were perfect. It was such a difficult pregnancy, but you were calm and easy from the first day." Her voice softens, like she's talking to a baby. "A lovable little angel, just like your brother had been. And you brought a miracle for Max. We had two wonderful little boys, two happy, healthy, smart little boys." She shakes her head. "It was too easy. Too easy. Too neat. Too perfect. All this time I've been waiting for the other shoe to drop." She leans over. Her hair, the dark brown color of my hair, Max's hair, obscures her face. "I guess it just did."

"I dress up in her clothes sometimes," Rachel says. She's sitting on the mattress. Cleo has squeezed under her knees and curled up there. "When nobody's at home. Or at night. I dress in her clothes, wear her perfume, dance around, and pretend I'm Karen. Then I see my reflection in the window, and sometimes I see someone coming up behind me, someone with an evil smirk and a knife, and I twist around, but there's nobody there. There's never anybody here. That's almost worse, you know. To wait, when you know you deserve what you fear, but it never comes." She looks at me. "That's why I came here."

"I don't understand."

"I saw Rook's picture on the news. And your picture. I saw how much you looked alike. I hoped you were like him."

She sounds annoyed. Like I disappointed her.

"When Rook was stalking Karen, I just wanted the problem to go away, and I thought it would if I closed my eyes and didn't know about it anymore. That's why I didn't tell anyone. Because I could get in trouble. Because my parents would freak if they knew what I'd done. Then Karen died. And it was my fault, and I still didn't tell anyone because I didn't want to get in trouble."

"Rook killed your sister. You didn't." It's easier to call him Rook. Rook has never stayed up with me late in the night, secretly watching a movie my parents wouldn't allow. Rook never gave me my favorite computer games or admired my computer graphics, telling me I was the best artist in the world. Rook is a monster. I can picture him. He's that sneering half elf, a bloody axe over his bare shoulder or a laser pistol strapped to his belt.

"Do you think she knew, before she died?" she asks. "Do you think she knew it was supposed to be me?"

"I don't know."

"Maybe he called her by my name." She's digging into her arm with her nails, twisting the skin, leaving it bruised and torn. "Maybe, when he cut her, he called her Lehcar, and she knew. She knew I used that name online. Do you think she told him he had the wrong sister? Maybe she knew, but she didn't tell him, so he wouldn't come after me next. Maybe she saved me. I set her up, and in return, she saved me."

My throat is dry. It's hard to speak. "You don't know that. Maybe—maybe it was the other way around. Maybe she even asked him to let her go and take you instead."

"I was the one who should have died. My parents will never forgive me. They always loved her best. She came first. Parents always love their first child more than the others." She turns her head to look at me. Her eyes are rimmed with red, but the cat is purring under her scarred hands, the furry belly bulging with the unborn kittens. "Like you. You were made to fix your brother. You'll always be second best."

"That's not true," I say. This is something I thought about a lot when I was little. Mom would tell me love was multiplied, not divided, or something like that. "Parents love their kids equally. It's not like you can measure love, anyway."

"You're wondering, aren't you? You're wondering why I pretended to be Karen."

"I guess . . ."

"I didn't mean to," she whispers. "I didn't mean to pretend to be Karen. I just wanted to be like Karen, and it just happened somehow."

"So Rook would like you." The words slip out. I didn't mean to say them. They're cruel. I expect Rachel to give me one of her scorching glares, but she doesn't. She rests her head on her knees and doesn't say anything.

She doesn't have to. The e-mails told me enough, and I can guess the rest. Rook liked girls his own age. College girls, not someone in junior high. Lehcar liked Rook. So Lehcar pretended to be what he wanted.

"It was supposed to be me."

Rachel rocks back and forth. She isn't looking good at all.

I don't know what to do. I wish Dad were here. Even though he's a full professor now, he does private practice on the side, because he loves to help people. I don't. I hate it when people are miserable because I don't know what to say or do at all. I don't even want to know about it. I just want to run away.

"Dad's a shrink," I say. "If you want to talk to him . . ."

Rachel looks at me like I suggested she emigrate to Alpha Centauri. "Talk. To your dad. To *Rook's* father."

At least she isn't shaking anymore.

"Forget it. Bad idea."

"Duh!"

Max's confession hits the news big-time that evening. The vultures return. The phones turn hyperactive again. And the next morning, when Mom and Dad come to my room, their faces tired and pale and hopeless, and they sit down on my bed and ask if I'd like to come with them to visit Max, I feel like I've suddenly gone mute. I don't know what to say. I don't even know what to think.

"He needs us, Josh," Mom says. She's clenching her hands and opening them, again and again, her face white and scared. I've never seen her like this. "If he did what he did, he's very, very sick. He can't help it."

"If he's sick, he should be in a hospital," I say. "Not in prison."

"Yes," Mom says. "He should be."

"It's not that black and white," Dad says. "You know that, Josh. Crime, sickness, evil—none of it is absolute. Not long ago, suicide was considered a crime. In the last century, homosexuality was an illness. Once, schizophrenia was demonic possession. Today, people are imprisoned for their crimes if we believe they know right from wrong but choose to do it anyway. Tomorrow we may decide they can't help it, that it isn't their fault, that they aren't responsible for their actions. It's all a matter of definition—"

"Jack, you're not in a lecture hall now!" Mom snaps. "This isn't a social studies class. This is our son's life."

Dad looks away.

"Max is sick," Mom continues. "We don't know yet what's wrong with him, but if he did this, he's very sick, and if he's confessing to something he didn't do, there's something wrong too. Either way, he needs our support. He could use your support too, honey. He asked about you yesterday. But we don't want to force you. If you feel uncomfortable visiting him, we'll understand. Max will understand," she adds, a little hesitantly. "It's up to you."

On the way to the jail, Mom's cell phone rings. It's Max's lawyer.

Max's former lawyer, as it turns out.

"Harris says Max fired him," Mom says. She stares in disbelief at her phone, looking at it from all directions, as if that will help. "He's hired someone new."

"What? Why? Who?" Dad asks.

"I don't know. Harris didn't know." Mom sighs, her breath trembling. "I'm sure Max will tell us."

When we get to the jail, the woman at the front desk points out Max's new lawyer, a tall, dark-haired man striding toward the exit. Mom and I go into the visiting room first, leaving Dad running after the new lawyer.

"Okay, honey." Mom pauses outside the door, puts her hands on my shoulders. The guard stops, his hand on the keypad. "Don't mention the charges," Mom continues. "We won't talk about the confession, the . . . crime. We'll just talk about everyday, normal things. That's what Max needs from us. Talk about your games, or school—no, not school, it will remind him why you're not going. TV, music . . . whatever. Try to act like nothing has happened."

"Okay."

Mom tries to smile, but it doesn't quite work. She

straightens her back and nods for the guard to open the door.

Max is already there. It's a different visiting room, but it looks identical to the first one. Max looks the same too. I don't know what I expected. That he'd be ashamed, maybe. Look guilty. But he's pretty much the same, only he seems a bit irritated. He jokes around with Mom, but he doesn't look at me at all.

How do you make small talk with a murderer?

I just sit there and let Mom do the chatting. Opposite my brother, the monster who killed Rachel's sister, who cyber-stalked dozens of girls. My brother, who confessed because of the evidence I discovered.

I'm the one who looks guilty and ashamed. He doesn't at all.

Behind us, the guard's phone beeps. I hear his footsteps recede a couple of steps as he answers.

Max leans over the table, ignores Mom who's talking about one of our favorite science fiction shows, and finally looks at me.

"Why?"

The word is flat. Big. It falls down on the table between us and grows, pulses.

I know what he's asking.

He knows. Somehow, he knows.

"Why what?" I ask, desperately trying to bluff, but Max isn't fooled.

"You're my brother. How could you betray me like that?"

I look at Mom. Dad didn't tell her where the information

came from. She doesn't know it was me. But her eyes widen as she realizes what Max must be talking about.

"I don't know what—"

He shakes his head impatiently, leans back. The cuffs rasp against the table. "Come off it, Josh. It's you. I knew right away it had to be you. You know Genesis Alpha. You know the system I have for my passwords. I don't know how you put it all together, how you found out about Rook, but I know it was you. And I won't forget this." He leans toward me again, looks deep into me, and I can't breathe anymore. His voice is calm. Too calm. "I will never forget this, Josh."

Mom is silent. She's not looking at me anymore, she's staring at Max with her mouth open, but she's not doing anything to stop him.

I'm afraid to look into his eyes now. There's something wrong inside his head, something horribly wrong, something that made him capable of doing what he did.

Would he do it to me?

Max glances at the guard, who's still talking into his phone by the door, watching us, but not listening. "I was about your age, you know," he says, his tone low. "When I first started wondering. You've got my eyes, my hair. We're so much alike. You'll start wondering too. Then you'll understand, baby brother. You'll understand."

"Max!" Mom chokes on his name. "Stop it . . . ," she whispers, and tears are leaking down her cheeks.

"I'm not like you," I force the words out, not because I need to tell Max, but because I need to tell myself.

Max doesn't take his eyes off me. He laughs. "You're more like me than you can imagine. You don't even want to look at me. Do you know why?" He leans across the table, toward me, but I still don't look. "It's because you're afraid you'll see yourself. We're the same. I look into your eyes, and it's like looking into a time-warped mirror. They made you for me, remember?" He tilts his head to the side. "You know, maybe they didn't even need for you to be born. They could have ripped the embryo apart to get the cells I needed. There was no need for a whole person. You're a by-product, little brother. Nothing more. I wouldn't still be alive without you, but you would never have existed at all if it weren't for me!"

He's yelling now. I feel dizzy. Mom puts her hand on my shoulder, pushing me back against the chair, away from Max. "Shut up!" she shouts. "Don't talk to your brother like that!"

The guard's heavy steps approach the table. Max looks up at him, leans back, raises his shackled hands in defeat. "Never mind. Peace."

Mom stands up. Pulls my arm until I'm standing. "Wait outside," she tells me, almost sobbing. "Wait outside, honey. I'll be right there."

I can't speak, so I nod.

"Sure. Leave. *You* can do that. Coward. Traitor. Look at me, Josh!"

I do. I look into his eyes, and I hold them. He stares at me without flinching. He doesn't look evil. He doesn't even look guilty. He looks angry and upset. He really does think I'm the one who did something wrong.

"I'll come after you," he says quietly. "Sooner or later. If I don't get you in this life, I will in the next. Because, you know, they may kill me, and it will be all your fault."

"Max!" Mom hisses. "How can you say those things? How could you . . ."

The guard walks closer. Puts his hand on my shoulder, turns me, pushing me toward the door. "That's enough, Mr. Seville," he says, and I look around for my father before realizing he's talking to Max.

Max looks up at the ceiling, shakes his head, ignores me as the guard pushes me out of the room.

I stand in the corridor, waiting for Mom. It seems dim and I feel alone, but in reality the fluorescent lights are bright and harsh, and there are uniformed people everywhere.

If I don't get you in this life, I will in the next.

I don't believe in ghosts anymore, but nevertheless, fear flutters inside me. An old fear of the dark resurrected, flashbacks to childhood terrors of skeletons rattling inside closets. Max laughed at me when I was five years old, when I wet the bed because I was afraid to leave it in the dark, terrified that if I put my feet on the floor, something would reach out and grab my bare ankles. His response embarrassed me, but it helped kill the fear too. Max made my fears seem childish and silly.

Max knows me. He knows everything about me.

I know nothing about him.

Thirteen

When I was little, I liked to dress like Max, talk like Max. I wanted to watch his movies, listen to his music, do everything just like him. Mom and Dad didn't approve. They wanted me to be independent, my own person, not a copy of my big brother.

But I worshipped him. I wanted to be just like him.

Now I want to be as different from him as I can. I tug on my hair and wish it would grow faster. That's what will help me the most. Long, shaggy hair, covering the face that looks too much like Max's face.

Of course you're different from me, I imagine Max saying. Like he's there in my head, answering my thoughts. *I bet you don't have the guts to kill someone even if you wanted to. Even in the computer games you always have to be the good guy. Hell, you always make* me *play the good guy!*

He's not wrong. I sometimes do evil stuff, but I prefer to rescue the good people and kill the bad people. It seems the way it's supposed to be. But it still means killing. Just killing the bad guys. And maybe that's no better. Maybe that's how

Max did it. Maybe he labeled Rachel and the other girls "bad guys." It's subjective, like Dad says. Even good and evil are a matter of definition.

I feel guilty. I feel guilty about turning Max in. I feel guilty about saving his life when I was born. I'd feel guilty, too, if I'd been born to save him and had failed. Mom and Dad feel guilty because they raised a monster and they think it's somehow their fault. Rachel feels guilty for not having saved her sister.

The only one who doesn't feel guilty is Max.

And he's the only one who did something really wrong.

Mom emerges from the visiting room, crying, and drags me off before they lead Max out of there. We run along the corridors like there's not enough air to breathe inside. When we're outside, Mom calls Dad, asks him to meet us at the car right away.

"What happened?" Dad says when he opens the car door and sees us huddled together, both of us still shivering. "Laura? Josh?"

Mom tells him, in jerky, incomplete sentences. "Why didn't you tell me, Jack? Why didn't you tell me Josh had found the evidence?"

Dad's gaze slides to me. "I guess I wanted to protect him. I told the police I'd discovered this . . ."

"You should have seen him." Mom's shivering even harder now. "You should have heard what he said to Josh, the way he said it, how he looked at him." Her lips are trembling. "It's not your fault, Josh. You did the right thing. You know that. Don't you?"

I don't answer. I don't know. I don't know anything.

■ ■ ■

Mom and Dad tiptoe around me the next morning, patting my shoulders, carefully asking if I feel like talking yet, but I shake my head and hunch over my breakfast.

"We'll be home early," Mom says. "Just a few morning meetings. Then we'll be home. We'll talk. Sort things out."

After they leave, I mope around for most of the morning. I play Genesis Alpha for a while, but it doesn't feel the way it normally does. Finally I find myself putting my boots and jacket on, although I don't know why I keep going out there.

There's a strange smell when I open the door to the shed. I pause before I open the screen door, sniffing cautiously and assuming the worst. But then I recognize it. I rush inside.

Rachel is sitting on the mattress, her back against the wall and a large cardboard box wedged between her knees. She looks up wide-eyed when she hears me rush in.

"Where have you been?" she snarls at me. She pushes herself into a kneeling position, holding on to the edges of the cardboard box.

I sink down on my knees on the mattress opposite her and bend over the box so our heads almost touch. "I was busy," I mutter, and can't help smiling when I look into the box. It's probably the first time I've smiled since Max's arrest.

They're tiny, blind, helpless. Five kittens on a bed of soft blue material. I wonder where Rachel got that blanket, but then I realize it's her sweater. Cleopatra purrs as her kittens suckle, but looks at us warily.

Rachel gestures at the kittens. "You left me to deal with this. Alone. Like I'm some kind of a cat midwife!"

"When did it happen?"

"It started early this morning. She lay down in that corner, in the pile of old newspapers, and started whining, woke me up. The first one just popped out. In a pool of slime and blood. Gross. Then they came one after another."

"Are they all out?"

"How the hell should I know?"

I stroke Cleo, prod her belly gently like Max taught me a long time ago. "Yeah. They're all here. It's a big litter for this queen."

"Queen?"

I remember the white queen she buried in Karen's grave and wish I hadn't used that word. "A mother cat in a breeding program is called a queen."

Rachel strokes a kitten with one finger, from the top of the head to the tip of the tiny tail. "I see. Does that mean the kittens are princes and princesses?"

The kittens have relaxed me. I laugh before I realize she isn't making a joke. Rachel doesn't make jokes. "No. Did the birth go okay?"

"How should I know? Nobody died, if that's what you're asking. One of the kittens was kind of stuck. Inside the bag they're born in. She tried to bite the bag, but she couldn't get it out. So I helped." She points. "That one."

I reach into the box and get Cleo's permission before lifting each kitten up. I never get used to how small they are. Each time,

I watch them grow bigger, and by the time the next litter comes around, I've forgotten how tiny they are in the beginning.

"You have to name them," I say, tucking the last kitten in by his mother. "The first person to see the kittens gives them names. It's a tradition."

Rachel has backed away from me. "What kind of names do kittens get?"

"Whatever you like."

"Do you sell them?"

"Yeah. To good homes. Mom's very picky about homes."

"Was she picky about Rook's home?"

I sigh. "Are you going to name the kittens?"

She looks at them contemplatively. "Yes. I think I will. Are they boys or girls?"

"The one you saved, the little blue one, is a girl. This sorrel one is a boy. The other three are girls."

"Why the weird names for the colors? Why don't you just call them gray and brown and orange?"

"I don't know. It's just the way it is."

"Where were you yesterday?"

"I visited Max."

Rachel doesn't say anything. She starts picking at the skin on the back of her hands, pinching the skin, twisting, digging her nails in until the small crescent-shape bruises start bleeding. Her fingernails are dirty. Probably from handling the newborn kittens.

"He knows," I say. "He wasn't supposed to find out, but he knows I turned him in."

"How?"

"He guessed. He's good at things like that." It's like he can read my mind, I almost say.

"What does he want from you?"

She doesn't ask what he said or what he did. It's a weird question. But an answer comes to mind immediately. My life. Max wants my life. After all, his life was the reason I was created. I'm the reason he's alive. I'm the reason he's confessed. In a way, everything's my fault. But I don't say any of that out loud. Instead I just shrug. "He thinks I'm a traitor. You know. Brothers aren't supposed to rat each other out."

"Like all he did was smoke a joint or steal a twenty?"

"Yeah. Like that."

Rachel looks into the box. "Is she okay?"

The blue kitten is having trouble suckling. Her brother and sisters are bigger and stronger, and she has been pushed into a corner. Her paws claw at the cardboard and her tiny blind face is scrunched up, her mouth gaping open, but she's so small I can't even hear the mewling sound she's trying to make.

I nudge her brother a bit to the side and place the blue kitten next to him, help her get the teat into her mouth. She calms under my hand, the tense body relaxing as she starts to drink.

"We have to watch out for her," I say. "For all of them. Make sure they all get plenty to drink."

"Rook said cats were the smartest creatures in the universe," Rachel says. "He said they get anything they want from their owners and never have to do anything in return except look cute."

"Did he talk about our cats?"

"Not that you bred them. Just that there were always cats around."

"Yeah. We got the first one when I was a baby. Moritz. He was Max's pet. A couple of years later Mom started to breed them."

"Rook has been in here," Rachel says. "I can feel it. I can feel evil has been inside here. He has been here, hasn't he?"

"Of course he has. He lived with us. Before he left for college, cleaning the litter boxes was his job. He was in this shed every day."

"Will your brother see when spring comes? Will he see the trees bloom and the grass get green?"

"Prisoners have the right to go outside. But I don't think there are a lot of trees there."

"My sister won't see anything," she snaps back. "She's rotting in her coffin. Why does he have the right to see anything?"

I don't know the answers to her questions, and I know that makes her mad. I wish I could answer them. I wish I could make everything right. I wish I could undo the terrible things my brother did. I almost wish I could take back the cells that cured him. It's a safe wish. It doesn't make me feel guilty, because it's impossible.

"When they made you, they made many fetuses. You were just one of many."

"Not fetuses," I correct. "Just a few cells at that stage. No brain, no organs, no body parts. Just a few identical cells."

"They were your brothers and sisters," Rachel continues mercilessly. "You were chosen—because you were the one most like Rook. The others were thrown away. Do you ever think about them? Your brothers and sisters, the ones who were not enough like Rook?"

This question has been there all my life. There are no right answers, but I've been placed on one side of the fence and there's no room for me on the other side. "They weren't my brothers and sisters. No more than the other billion eggs inside my mother were."

"They were cells, dividing to make a person. Like you were. That's what we are, aren't we? Even now, we're nothing but a bunch of multiplying cells. What's the difference between us and them?"

"We have minds. We think. We feel. We're human."

"We kill. We torture. We rape. We're human."

Rachel mimics my voice. I sound tired, unconvincing, like I'm spouting lines someone taught me a long time ago. I see the challenge in Rachel's eyes. She wants to fight. She doesn't care what we fight about, as long as we fight.

"Tell me about Karen," I say.

"Why?"

"Because I'm sick of talking about Max or myself all the time."

She looks down at the kittens between us. Her grasp on the edge of the cardboard box tightens. "It's like everybody died," she says. "When Karen died. My parents are different people now. My old parents are gone, just like Karen is gone. I'm gone too. Everything's different. The whole world is a different color."

I nod, because I know what she means. My parents have also changed in the last few days. It's not just that they're sad and angry and afraid, it's more like everything about them is different. I guess that's what they mean by life-changing events.

"Karen was missing for nine days," Rachel says. "Her roommate called when she hadn't seen her for two days. Mom started calling everyone. Everyone. After that, she called the police. But it was still seven more days until they found her." She starts chewing on her finger, but spits and grimaces when she realizes how dirty it is. "I thought about Rook while she was missing. I thought about Rook a lot. I wanted to log on and ask him. I wanted to make sure I was just being paranoid. But I didn't. And I never saw my sister again. They couldn't have an open casket at her funeral. Her face was too damaged. All of her was too damaged."

I shut my eyes, but open them quickly again because the images are stronger behind closed lids. Rachel's voice isn't even quivering. It's like she's said this a hundred times before.

"I was glad the casket was closed. I'd never seen a dead body. Only Dad saw her. Three months ago now. Since then, he's been drinking every night. Not that he's a drunk or anything. He just needs it so he can sleep. He doesn't go to bed anymore. He sits in front of the television and falls asleep there. We never turn it off. But it doesn't help much. He still wakes up screaming. Or crying. I didn't know my dad could cry like that.

"He sees Karen in the morgue when he dreams. I do too. I don't know what she looked like, but I see her. Sometimes it's not her on that slab. Sometimes it's me. Sometimes I feel the cuts all over me, feel the blood on my face, pain everywhere from what he did to me, and I can't move because I'm dead. And I'm glad. Relieved. In the dream I think about Karen, and I'm glad it was all a nightmare and she isn't dead, after all. Instead I'm the one who's dead and everything happened the way it was supposed to happen."

Rachel picks up one of the kittens, lies back on the mattress, the tiny animal sprawled on her chest. She stares up at the ceiling. "Mom didn't see her. Dad asked her not to. He thought it would be for the best. But I think it would have been better, you know? Because Mom wakes up screaming too."

Her breath, when she inhales deeply, trembles, but her voice does not. "What you imagine is always worse than the truth." She lifts her head and her gaze fastens on mine. Green. Blue. I'm never sure. "Isn't it?"

Fourteen

"Maybe Max is sick," I tell Rachel later on, after we've spoiled Cleopatra with tuna and Rachel has given the kittens names. They're all royalty. The little blue one, Rachel's favorite, is Princess. I have no idea how I'll explain their names to Mom and Dad. "Maybe there's something wrong with his brain so that he's not able to feel guilty."

"You feel guilty after you do something. Or don't do something. Not before. It doesn't stop you from doing horrible things."

"Maybe you stop because you know it will make you feel guilty."

Rachel shakes her head. "It doesn't make sense. Maybe that's a part of it, but it can't be all there is to it."

"You feel guilty because you know what's right and wrong."

"Rook knows killing is wrong. Doesn't he?"

I nod. "I think so. He just doesn't care. He wants to do it, so he doesn't care if it's wrong. He just wants to, so he does."

"But there's something crazy in wanting to do something

like that. Knowing what's right and wrong is what should stop you, but what makes you want to do it in the first place?"

We stare at each other. We're asking questions that have no answers.

"Rook likes hurting people," Rachel says. "People like him want to know that their victims suffer. He probably wouldn't even have bothered to kill her if she hadn't suffered. It wouldn't be any fun that way. It wouldn't be any fun to kill a person in their sleep."

Thinking about what Max did, how he did it, gives me the shivers. An icy feeling inside, and the urge to squeeze my eyes shut, tighter and tighter until I can't see anything but random explosions of color.

"I want to figure it out," Rachel says, "where evil comes from. If I want to become an expert in evil, what should I study?"

"I don't know."

"Would it be biology or psychology or law or philosophy?"

"Probably a bit of everything."

Rachel laughs. I don't like the sound of her laughter. It's like a mechanical noise. Like a laughing doll in a toy store, when you push a button or pull a string or activate it with a shouted command. "Yeah. Perhaps I should major in a bit of everything."

I feel foolish. "I just meant—"

"I know what you meant." Her tone is patronizing again and I hate that, I hate it when people make me feel stupid. I clench my fists because I want to yell at her and I can't. I feel like slamming my fist against the wall and I can't. I feel like grabbing her and shaking her and shoving her out the door, but I can't. I won't. I won't do any of that. So I wait, and let Rachel play her game.

"Maybe the only way is to learn by doing," she says. "Do you think that's it? Do you have to become evil to understand evil?"

"I don't know."

"You said evil is human. Cruelty is human. Human is intelligence. So it makes sense that cruelty stems from intelligence. Maybe it's a side effect of intelligence."

"Maybe."

"Do you know your own IQ?"

"No," I lie. I do know. It's one of the things Dr. Ashe has in her files, and last time I demanded to know the results. But I'm not going to give Rachel a number to tag me with.

"I bet it's pretty high." Rachel looks at me, calculating, and I don't trust her one bit. "For you and Rook both. Both your parents are scientists. So you've got smart genes."

"Genes aren't everything."

"Aren't they?"

"No. They're not."

Rachel lines up two tiny kitten tails, gently loops them around each other. Blue and sorrel. "You breed cats. For color and looks."

"Yeah."

"And personality. Behavior. So they make good pets." She looks at me when I don't answer. "Right?" she snarls.

"Right."

"You can do that because the way they look and the way they act is in their genes. So when you breed a king with a queen, you know what you get."

"No. We don't know. We can affect the odds because we are familiar with the gene pool of each parent, but we don't know."

"Yeah. Odds. Like the odds of you and Rook being alike."

"Or you and your sister."

"Karen wasn't always a very nice sister."

I consider telling her Max isn't the best of brothers.

"When I was little, I loved to play with Karen. But she didn't like playing with me. I was such a baby, she said. She didn't want me touching her stuff, either. But I still thought she was the most fantastic person in the universe. Big sister. Nobody was cooler, smarter, prettier." Rachel tosses me a cat toy, a spongy ball she's dug up from behind the mattress, and gestures for me to throw it back. "Is that what you thought about your brother?"

"I guess."

"He's a lot older than you are."

"Yeah."

"Big brother. So he must have been your idol. Your hero. Right?"

"Yeah."

Rachel smiles. Like she's won a victory. Her teeth don't show. Her lips are dry, chapped. I think she gnaws on them, like on her fingers.

"You look a lot like him on the outside. You must be similar on the inside too. You must think like him. Feel like him. If you have any feelings at all."

The walls seem too close and I want to lash out at Rachel again, punish her like she's punishing me. It's stupid to feel trapped. Max is the caged animal, not me. I'll never be like him. I won't let it happen. I stand up. Reach out with my arm, steady myself against the wall and look defiantly down at Rachel. "No. I'm not a killer."

Rachel is leaning back against a big bag of cat litter. She holds a kitten to her cheek, and she looks cute and sweet and normal for a moment. Then the rubber mask is back. It stretches as she smiles at me. "Not yet."

She's so damn good at this. I give in to the fear and the fury and leave the shed, slamming the door on Rachel's cackle. I'm not like Max. I'll never be like Max.

In the morning Mom is putting down the phone as I trudge down the stairs. She hurries toward the television and rummages around for the remote. "Jack!" she calls, and Dad emerges from his study. "It's Diane. She was watching the news—Max's new lawyer is on the morning show. Costello. On television. Now."

"Costello?" Dad repeats. He removes his glasses and polishes them with the loose hem of his cotton shirt, puts them back on, and peers at the blank TV screen. "About Max? Why?"

Mom switches on the television. Max's face fills the screen. By now we should be used to it, but Mom winces.

"What's going on?" Dad asks, but nobody has an answer for him. He grabs the phone, but before he can dial anywhere, the new guy, Dan Lione, appears on the television, sitting in an armchair next to the famous talk show host. In front of them, a small audience. Cameras visible in the background.

"I don't like that guy," Dad mutters. "He's a sleazebag. He just took Max on hoping to milk some media attention out of the case. Max should have kept Richard Harris."

"It's Max's choice," Mom says. "He's an adult, after all. . . ."

"But what the hell are they—"

Mom shushes Dad as Mr. Lione starts talking.

"Thank you for this opportunity, Mr. Costello," he says to the host. "I really appreciate getting this chance to tell you my client's story."

Mr. Costello leans back. "The audience is all yours, Dan."

The camera zooms in on Mr. Lione, away from the talk show host. For long moments he gazes out over the audience, and an excited murmur starts. When it dies down and there's silence, he starts talking.

Dad drops into a chair. Mom falls onto the sofa. I sit down silently on a chair in a corner behind them, barely daring to breathe for fear they'll tell me to go to my room and make me miss this. "I'd like to tell you a story," the lawyer says. "A story of a little boy. I want you to listen carefully. It's a long story, but it has a very important point."

On the screen behind him a picture shimmers into life. It's a childhood picture of Max, sick in his hospital bed, looking tiny and pathetic.

"This is Max. He's five years old. Max has cancer. For three years, Max has fought. As long as he can remember, he has fought. His allies are alien chemicals ravaging his body, radiation burning his insides, a scalpel slicing through his flesh. But no treatment has worked. Nothing works. Max is dying."

Pictures flash on the screen in a slow slideshow. Max with tubes stuck to him everywhere. Max in surgery. Max in chemo. Max in isolation. Max smiling while Dad opens a birthday present for him, but too weak to hold his head up, let alone his toys.

"Where did he get these pictures?" Dad asks angrily.

"I e-mailed him some photos," Mom murmurs.

"You did what?"

"He called me yesterday, asked for some childhood pictures of Max. He said he might need them for the defense. That it would help if the jury saw how ill Max was . . . all the pain and misery he suffered . . . how that must have scarred him . . ." Mom's voice trails off. "I thought he was on our side! I didn't dream he'd use them like this! How could this possibly help his defense?"

Lione continues while the photographs keep flashing on the screen. "Max grew up with death. As long as he can remember, he's been surrounded by death. He makes friends at the hospital, only to watch them quietly disappear. At first he asks about them. Then he doesn't. By the time Max is six years old, he has decided he wants a cremation. He wants his ashes scattered to the wind. When he is seven years old, he's ready to die. He's been sick as long as he can remember. He's in constant pain. He's unable to play like other little children. Stuck in a bed, sometimes too weak to even smile at his favorite cartoons, he watches as his parents have already started to grieve. Sometimes he feels they are waiting for it to be over. Waiting for him to die."

Mr. Lione takes a slow, deliberate drink of water. Looks up, smiles. A new picture flashes on the screen. It's me. A baby, beside Max in the hospital bed. Max is looking at me. My hand is around two of his fingers.

"Then, a miracle. A miracle of science. A baby brother. A brother carefully chosen. A baby brother whose tissues match his, a brother whose cells can cure Max. A brother created to heal him. And the miracle works. Max receives his brother's healthy cells, and he starts getting better. He's in remission. Soon there is no trace of the disease anymore. The doctors are optimistic that it will never return. His brother has cured him. Max can play outside. He can have a pet. He can go to birthday parties. He can make friends and they don't die on him. He can do anything now. Life is perfect. But . . ."

Mr. Lione pauses.

"Max is jealous, too. Of course he is. It's only normal. His parents are preoccupied with the new baby, now that Max is healthy. The baby is more needy now. He takes up their time, their attention."

Dad shifts in his seat, looks at Mom. "Where is he going with this? Is he saying we neglected Max after Josh was born?"

Mom doesn't take her eyes off the screen.

"Then one weekend, Max gets sick," the lawyer continues. "He's weak. He has a fever. He throws up. His parents are terrified. They leave his little brother with a neighbor and rush Max to the hospital. More tests. More needles. Another white hospital bed and doctors with eyes Max doesn't trust anymore. But he's fine. It's just a flu, the doctors say, smiling at Mom and Dad. Nothing to worry about.

"That evening Max sneaks down the stairs. He's an intelligent and inquisitive little boy. He wants to—he needs to—know everything. He wants to know every detail about his disease, and if he's really dying, he wants to know that, too. Sometimes his parents and the doctors have tried to hide the facts from him. Did he really just have the flu—or are his parents trying to protect him from the truth?

"He's done this before. He'll sit on the bottom stair and listen to their voices drift to him, and he'll learn about his blood count, his prognosis, all the things they won't tell him in person. But this time, they aren't talking about him. They're talking about Josh. His baby brother.

"Max isn't very interested in their conversation about Josh. But he sits there for a while, listening, growing more and more confused by what they're saying. It's then that he hears the word for the first time."

The lawyer pauses. Dad looks at Mom. Mom looks at Dad. They both look back at me. Mom shakes her head. Dad shoves both hands through his short hair. "What—" he says.

"It can't be," Mom says. "It's not possible."

On the television screen, the lawyer is again taking a drink of water. The host is silent. This is Mr. Lione's moment. Whispers spread across the studio. A feeling of dread crawls up my spine. "Max holds his breath," the attorney says, almost whispering, and the room falls completely silent. "He keeps listening. He moves closer, so he doesn't miss a word. They're still talking about his little brother, Josh. Josh, who is a designer baby, created to heal Max. But Josh is more than that. Josh is the *perfect* designer baby."

The lawyer pauses. Once again he brings the glass to his lips and sips water. "Max's mother is a biologist," he continues. "Dr. Seville works at one of the best research facilities in the country. She works with world-renowned scientists. A new law has been passed, stopping them from continuing their research. They are disgruntled. Some of them are furious. Their lives' work has been stopped, just as they're on the cusp of many important breakthroughs. Their lives' work—which could save so many lives. Including the life of Dr. Seville's little boy."

Dad is leaning over, his elbows on his knees, his knuckles in his eyes. Mom's hands hover over her ears, like she doesn't want to hear what the lawyer is saying. I slide down in my seat, but although I want to escape, I can't bring myself to run away.

"Whose idea is it? Who's the first to voice it? The mother? One of her colleagues? It doesn't matter. The result does matter. The result is there. The result saved Max's life."

My picture flashes on the screen behind the lawyer. It's

side by side with an old picture of Max. Mr. Lione looks straight into the camera, and I recoil as the illusion of television makes our eyes meet.

"A clone," the lawyer says. "That's their solution. That's Max's cure."

Fifteen

I laugh, because it's too ridiculous. I can't help it. I look at Dad, wanting him to shake his head in disbelief at what the man is saying. But he doesn't. He stares at the lawyer, his jaw clenched. Mom's face is white.

On the television, Mr. Lione continues, and I'm vaguely surprised because I feel like the whole world should be frozen still right now.

"Max's baby brother is one of the first human clones in history. Perhaps the very first. But it's a secret. What they did wasn't exactly legal. Not exactly ethical. That's what their parents talk about while Max listens. The importance of keeping this a secret. A secret forever. It is never to be mentioned again. Not even between the two of them. The boys will never find out. The world will never find out.

"Max is a smart boy. From his hospital bed he has watched countless hours of television, read hundreds of books. He knows what a clone is. He knows what it means. Max sneaks back upstairs, and his parents never know he was there. He crawls into his bed, shivering, even though it's not cold. He thinks about his baby brother, asleep in the nursery next to their parents' bedroom, his old room. It dawns on him what this means. His parents got a new baby, not only to heal him. They also got a replacement, in case the cure didn't work. They have a new Max. An identical child, this one without the disease. This one will grow strong and healthy. This new Max will be the child they wanted—and it no longer matters whether Max lives or not."

"No . . . no . . . no . . ." It's Mom's voice. She's barely moving her lips, but I hear her. "Oh, Max . . . no . . ."

"That night Max closes his eyes and meets darkness. He sees himself walking into the nursery. He sees himself holding a pillow over the baby's face, until the new Max stops moving. He fantasizes about reclaiming his rightful spot in his parents' hearts. It is the first of many fantasies. It is Max's first journey into the shadows that later will consume him."

The lawyer pauses. He looks away from the camera, down at his notes, then at Mr. Costello.

"Fascinating. Chilling," Mr. Costello says. "But I must confess, hard to believe. It sounds like science fiction. Do you have any proof? And how will this help with Mr. Seville's defense?"

"I know it sounds unbelievable," Mr. Lione says. "It *is* unbelievable. But it's not science fiction. It's science fact, and it really shouldn't be that surprising. We've had the technology for a while—of course someone, somewhere has taken advantage of it. Imagine the psychological devastation for a young child. Imagine the scars on his psyche. And we have seen the heartbreaking consequences. . . ."

"But can you prove any of this?"

"Yes, quite easily." He looks into the camera and our eyes meet again. "All we need is a cell sample from the cloned child."

The cloned child.

That's me.

I feel dizzy. Almost like that time when I was little and fell from the swings and got a big gash on my head. I lost so much blood I nearly passed out. That's how it feels. Like there's no blood left in my head anymore, like there's nothing in there at all.

Mom's lips are pinched white. Dad's face is red. Neither of them is looking at me.

"Is it true?" I ask, but nobody hears me. Maybe I didn't say it loud enough. "Is it true?" I ask, standing up. "Is it true?" I yell. My fists are clenched, and when I feel my nails dig into my palms, feel the bite of it rush through my numb system, I almost understand why pain is Rachel's friend.

My mother looks absent and tired, like the answer doesn't matter anymore. Her eyes are on the television where Mr. Lione is still answering Mr. Costello's questions. "Yes, Josh. It's true."

I can't breathe. Dad sits me down. His arm is heavy over my shoulder, and he says something, but I hear nothing. Blood is rushing through my head again and then I'm breathing hard, as if I've just run a long way.

"Josh?" Dad's saying when I start hearing again. His hands are warm on my cheeks, holding me steady, and I realize I'm shaking hard. "It's okay. Everything will be okay. I promise."

"How can it be okay? How can it ever be okay, Dad?"

"Nobody was supposed to know," Mom whispers. "Ever."

"Max has always known," I say. Dad's hands slide away from my face when I twist around to look at Mom. "Since he was little. Since I was a baby. Max has always known. He has always hated me, hasn't he?"

Mom moves closer, tries to hug me, but I hold out my hands and stop her. She shakes her head. "Max always seemed to love you. I don't know what he has been thinking, Josh. I just don't know."

Clone. *Clone.* The word is like something from a foreign language, and I keep playing it in my head over and over again, as if I've misunderstood its meaning. "This is why Dr. Di keeps testing me. I'm her secret science project."

"It wasn't like that."

"I'm a lab animal!" I yell. "I'm not even my own person! I'm a *clone.* I'm a backup! I'm reserve parts! I don't even matter! Why else wouldn't you even tell me anything? Why else would you lie about what I am?"

Dad's arm tightens around my shoulders, softening the impatient tone of his voice. "Josh, don't. It's not like that. You're too smart to leap to such paranoid conclusions."

"You just admitted it! I'm a clone of Max! What other conclusion is there?"

Dad mutes the television. "Think about it, Josh. You know what a clone is. Biologically you're Max's identical twin. That's all. It isn't any more sinister than that."

Dad can make anything sound rational and normal. But

this isn't rational and normal. I'm a clone of my brother, and my brother is a psychopathic killer. If this were no big deal, my brother and I would not be on television under a "Breaking News!" header.

"Are there others? Are there other clones?"

"We don't know," Dad says. "It's possible that somewhere in the world there are laboratories where—"

"I mean me. Are there more of me?"

Dad almost laughs, startled. "Oh, no. Of course not."

"Why not?" I yell. "Why not make a whole army of spare parts for Max? Why not just cut me up and pickle my organs into jars? You never know when Max is going to need one!"

I look at the television screen. They've gone on to explain the cloning process. "What happens to me now?" My voice is thin and scared, and Dad holds me tighter. I shove his arms away, stand up. "What's going to happen to me now?"

"What do you mean, honey?" Mom asks. She reaches out to me again, but I refuse to take her hand. "Nothing will happen to you, Josh. We won't let anything happen to you."

"I'm him! I have his genes!"

"You have *our* genes, son," Dad says. "That's what you have. Genetically speaking, you're a mixture of me and your mother. But when it really comes down to it, you're you."

I stand there, between them, and I know both of them want to put their arms around me, want to assure me everything will be okay, and although that's what I desperately need to hear, I back off from them. I've had enough of lies. I fold my arms on my chest, grabbing each upper arm tight. Tighter. Squeezing until it hurts. "I'm the same as Max. And Max is—"

"It doesn't matter what Max is," Dad says. "That doesn't say anything about you."

"You boys have always been different in many ways, Josh," Mom says. Her voice is trembling. "Surprisingly different, considering you are twins."

"Clones."

"Twins," Mom insists. "Twins born a few years apart, with some scientific help. That's all."

"That's not *all*, Mom, and you know it. That's just another lie! Were you ever going to tell me?"

They share a look. "No," Dad finally says. "To be honest, no. We weren't."

"Never?"

"No. Well, not for the foreseeable future, anyway."

"Why?"

"We thought it would be best. For you. For Max. There's so much superstition and prejudice in the world, so much ignorance. We wanted to protect you from the fallout." Dad sighs. "And now it looks like we're about to find out just how bad it can get."

"We'll deny it," Mom says. "We'll deny everything, and they can't force you to give a DNA sample."

"I wouldn't count on it," Dad mutters. "What we did was illegal, remember? We can be prosecuted."

I'm illegal. I'm like crack cocaine or polygamy. Outlawed.

If Mom and Dad get in trouble over this, I'll be exhibit A for the prosecution.

There is silence, for how long I don't know. I almost want to laugh. "You should have told me," I say instead. Because that matters. "Even if you told nobody else, I had a right to know."

"It wasn't safe, Josh," Mom says, her voice broken, tears once more erupting from her eyes. "Please understand. Kids tell each other secrets. They tell their girlfriends, who tell their best friends, who tell . . . Secrets have a way of getting out. It simply wasn't safe. There's so much fanaticism out there, and the press—we wanted you to grow up in peace. Both of you. We are so sorry, but please try to understand, we only wanted what was best for you."

All at once, our phones are ringing. The home phone, Mom's cell phone, Dad's cell phone and mine, where they lie in a jumble on the small dresser near the front door.

"I'm going upstairs," Mom says. "Make some calls. I need to talk to Diane. This affects her, too . . ."

Dad and I are left alone together. He's limp in his chair, staring at his wedding ring, rubbing it with his thumb.

"You let me think I was a designer baby. That I was selected as an embryo because I matched Max. You told me this whole story about how I was created, and it was all a lie. . . ."

"It was a true story, Josh. It was what we went through to have you."

"You didn't get me that way."

"It was a part of the process of getting you. We tried for so long. Do you know how it's done?"

Of course I know. They told me how. They *lied* to me how.

"They gave your mother hormones. To stimulate her eggs. So they could harvest many eggs at once. The number varied. Sometimes there were as little as four eggs, sometimes twenty. Then they'd use my sperm to impregnate the eggs."

"Just like fish," I interject. Dad looks at me, frowning. "Fish. Many fish species. The female fish lays the eggs, then the male fish comes along after the fact and fertilizes them."

Dad stares at me. "I suppose it was a bit like that. Anyway, we tried it that way. The fish way. For more than a year. Meanwhile, Max was dying. This was his only hope."

"How many embryos did you make?"

Dad shakes his head. "I don't know. Dozens and dozens. Only two of them were compatible, but we lost both. Your mother didn't tolerate the stress very well. Or the hormones. She started to obsess about all the embryos we couldn't use. It was a terrible time for all of us." He sighs, rubs his face with his hands. "Max was dying. A part of Laura seemed to die with every failed attempt. Then, well . . ."

"Enter Dr. Die-Hard."

For once Dad doesn't scold me for using the nickname. "The lab was close to the children's hospital, and Diane would frequently look in on Max for us. We couldn't stay with him as much as we'd have liked while we were involved in the IVF treatment. One morning she was sitting there with him when your mother arrived. He was asleep. Your mother sat down next to him and started crying. We'd lost a baby that night. Again. She'd carried him only seven weeks."

"I cried," Mom says, startling us both. She's standing in the doorway, her hand clutching the shirt at her stomach. "I held Max's hand, and I sobbed for the baby I'd lost, the one I'd lost before, and the child I was about to lose, the innocent little boy sleeping in that hospital bed, almost comatose from the cocktail of drugs they gave him to ease the pain. Diane was there. She understood. She lost her little girl to a brain tumor the year Max was born. She's always understood. I told her I couldn't do it anymore. I couldn't let them continue creating all those embryos and then throwing them away because they didn't match. But saying that also meant giving up on Max. It meant letting Max die. I couldn't do that, either."

Mom falls into the chair next to Dad. She reaches out and their hands entwine.

"'There is another way,' Diane told us." Mom is whispering now. "'You know there is another way. With our new method we could do it, and it would be quicker and more effective than IVF. But it's not legal. Not now. Not yet. We have the technology, we could save Max's life, but there is a law against it.'" She shakes her head. "Once the suggestion was there, out in the open, once Diane had assured us they could clone Max and create a viable embryo, guaranteed to match, we didn't think twice. What parent cares about the law when their child's life is at stake? There was no other way. There was no guarantee that the pregnancy would be successful, but if it succeeded, we'd have a cure for Max, and we'd have another child. And we knew we'd love our new little boy just as much as we loved Max."

"But if I'm identical to Max . . . how could you be sure I wouldn't get sick too?"

"We couldn't be sure," Dad says. "Max's type of cancer . . . when one identical twin falls ill, there's a fifteen percent chance the other one will too. For you, the risk was smaller because you were born years apart and your environmental factors were different. It was a risk we decided to take."

"For Max."

Dad meets my eyes. His are damp, and his voice isn't steady anymore. "There was a chance that whatever caused Max to get sick would also happen to you. Because you share the same DNA, you body chemistry is similar, your immune systems, your vulnerabilities. But the chances of you being healthy were better. Instead of one dying little boy, we'd have two healthy ones."

"And it wouldn't matter anyway, because even if I got sick later on, I'd already have healed Max. I'd already have served my purpose."

"No, Josh. It was not like that."

Out of the corner of my eye I see Rachel's face flash on the television screen. I grab the remote and turn the sound up.

Rachel's parents are there, live from their home. Their eyes are red-rimmed, and angry lines arch around their mouths. Behind them, pictures of Rachel and Karen hang on the wall.

"Something must be done," Rachel's mother says. She pushes the back of her hand against her mouth, shakes her head. The camera zooms in on her, then moves to her husband.

"We can't take the chance," he says. "One of our daughters is dead, the other one is missing. Karen died in the most horrible way. If there's a chance this boy could become a monster like his brother, we must act. If there's a possibility he can turn into a killer, that he will torture and murder innocent people, something must be done."

"But he hasn't done anything," the reporter said. "Can we justify incarcerating an innocent child?"

"We don't let tiger cubs loose in the city, do we? There must be institutions for people who are dangerous. Not a prison, just a place where he's watched, where he can't do something like this. He can have a good life there. And the rest of us can be safe."

"Of course it isn't fair," Rachel's mother interjects. "We know that. It's unfair to the boy. He hasn't done anything—yet. But our daughter's death wasn't fair either. The boy is only a child now, but when he grows up . . . who knows what will happen? Who knows what kind of evil is inside him? We have to watch him carefully." She looks into the camera. "Please, don't let this happen a second time. That boy could be a time bomb. Next week, next month, ten years from now, he may strike. We have the duty to protect ourselves. To protect our children."

"There are alternatives to imprisonment," Rachel's father says. "A security guard. One of those ankle bracelets. So we know where he is, what he's doing, at all times."

"Unbelievable," Dad breathes. "I know their little girl is still missing, but still, this is unbelievable. Turn it off."

"No. I want to see this."

"Why, Josh?" Dad sounds exhausted underneath the anger and fear. Mom's just sitting there beside him, not speaking, not moving. Her eyes are on the television, but I don't think she's seeing much.

"They're talking about me. I'm interested."

"It's nonsense. You know it's nonsense."

"We don't know that yet. Max wasn't a killer when he was my age. You don't know what made him that way. You can't be sure about anything. You don't know about me yet. *I* don't know about me yet!"

"Josh, if you and Max were identical twins, born at the same time, this would not be happening!" Dad shouts. "And identical twins is all you are. If the Crosse parents would stop for a moment, look up from their grief, they'd realize that."

I take a deep breath. "I want to see Max. Today. Now. Can we visit him?"

"Josh . . ." Dad frowns. "That's not a good idea. Right now, Max wants to hurt you. He wants to hurt everybody."

"He's doing this because I turned him in."

Dad hesitates. Nods. "That would be my guess too."

"I need to see him."

"Why?"

I shake my head hard and turn away. I'm not sure why. I only know I have to.

Maybe I have to look into his eyes to see if I find myself.

Sixteen

Max is looking different today. Happy. Pleased with himself.
He looks at me instantly. Not at Mom and Dad. Only at me.
There's a light in his eyes I have never seen before.

"Hey," he says as I sit down between my parents. "Big
news, huh?"

I look at my brother and I feel almost faint. I believe it, but
I still don't. It's too incredible.

"Convenient, wasn't it?" Max laughs. He's still looking at
me. Only me. Straight into my eyes. Deep into me. "Not only
did they get me a blood donor, marrow donor—heck, an
organ donor if I needed one, but they also got an identical
baby. A replacement for me if I died. They couldn't lose. It
must have been perfect."

"It was never like that, son," Dad says. Mom has started
crying again. She tries to say something but can't.

"Sure it was, Dad," Max says, but still doesn't take his eyes
off me.

"I'm sorry if that's what you thought, Max. But it was
never like that. Josh was never meant to replace you."

"Dr. Die-Hard must have been ecstatic. Her own personal laboratory right here. Haven't you noticed the way she looks at you, Josh? You're the star of her career. It must be driving her nuts that she can't make you public, can't show you off like a prize lab rat. She's written journal articles about you, you know. About both of us. She can't publish them, of course. At least, not yet. But she can pass them around to like-minded colleagues."

"How do you know about these articles, Max?" Dad asks.

Max answers, but he doesn't look away from me. "Not hard to find. They're in her computer."

"You broke into her office."

Dad's the one who spoke, but it's me Max grins at. "You should be able to find them. Inside one of the computer magazines in my old room. I knew Mom and Dad would never flip through those, but, well, I rather thought some day you might. Anyway, Diane must be thrilled now. Her little project just took a very interesting turn. She'll want to watch you develop. Watch you become more and more like me. Will you become a 'psychopath' too? Will you kill someone?" He leans forward. "What will happen to you now, Josh? We're identical. What will happen to you now that everybody knows you're another me?"

"Just because we have the same genes, that doesn't mean we're the same," I force out. "DNA is not a killer."

Max chuckles. "Is that like saying guns don't kill?"

"You killed someone. I didn't."

"Are you sure? Maybe there is no you and me. Maybe there's only we."

Mom is crying at my side. She pushes her chair backward, stands up, and I hear the locks rattle as the guard lets her out of the room.

"Josh . . ." Dad puts his hand on my arm. "This is enough. Go with your mother."

"No," I say, shrugging his hand off. "I'm talking to my brother."

"Look at that," Max drawls. "Little Josh, standing up to Mom and Dad. Who'd have thought? I'm so proud. My liberator. My savior. My cure. My clone."

"Why are you doing this?" Dad yells.

Max doesn't look away from me, ignores Dad. "I'm sorry, Josh," he says, smiling to show he's not sorry at all. "This is my one trump card. My sad past. My unique childhood. My scarred psyche, the irretrievable damage to my personality. Lione says that might make all the difference to my sentence and to my chances of parole. And remember, *brother*, this is your destiny, so you can hardly complain. You were put on this Earth to rescue me." His eyes narrow, spit fire for a second before he's smiling again. "You forgot that when you turned me in. You'll never forget now. I'm the original. You're just an imitation."

"Why did you do it?" I ask. I dare, now. "Why did you kill Karen?"

Max seems to explode in anger. He slams his fists down so the table shakes, and he finally looks away from me and at Dad instead. "I should have died! You shouldn't have played God and cloned me!"

Dad leans forward, reaches out to him, but pulls his hand back. "We loved you, Max. We couldn't bear the thought of losing you. Where do you draw the line? When should we have stopped trying to save your life? What about your shots? Antibiotics for your infections? The medicine when you first became ill? The radiation treatment? At what point should we have given up and let you die?"

Max shakes his head. "You don't understand. And it doesn't matter, anyway. I'm famous now. We'll make headlines all over the world. People will write books about me, movies. They'll make TV documentaries, write hundreds of academic papers. Years from now they'll still be interviewing you, asking questions about me."

Dad shakes his head sadly. "Max . . . you know that's ridiculous."

Max leans towards me and sniffs, a distant look in his eyes. "You haven't started smoking, have you, Josh?"

I shake my head.

"You smell like cigarettes."

Rachel's cigarettes. Of course. It's a wonder my parents haven't noticed. "Must have walked through a cloud of smoke somewhere in the hallway." I wonder if he recognizes the smell as Karen's cigarettes, if she smelled of them as he killed her, and I can't help it, I shudder violently.

Max's gaze fastens on me, chafes across my face. "What's wrong?"

"Nothing. I'm a little cold, that's all."

It's like he's two people. My brother, the brother I've always known, and a monster, a stranger, together in one person, shimmering together and apart. Good and evil. It isn't as simple as it is inside Genesis Alpha. It isn't as simple as I always thought it was.

"Do you think we share a soul, Josh? Seeing as how you were made from me?"

My soul is my own, no matter why or how I was created. I have to believe that. I stare straight back into Max's eyes and shake my head. Max laughs. He looks away. Rubs his forehead with his shackled hands. They are shaking.

"I'm afraid of dying," he says suddenly. "That's why I confessed. Hoping to avoid the death penalty. I'm not afraid of death. Not of hell or anything. I don't believe in heaven or hell. But the moment of dying. That moment when you realize you're dying . . . when the final hope vanishes and your vision starts to narrow . . . when you know you're fading out. It happened to me a few times back then, you know. They brought me back every time. Back to sickness and pain and the eternal wait for the cure. A cure. Mom kept promising me a cure." He looks at me again. "Are you afraid of dying?"

I guess I am, but I haven't thought about it a lot. I've thought about Max's death, Karen's death. But not my own.

"If I'm executed, part of you will die with me. The part they injected into me. It will rot in the ground with me. Maybe I should get cremated like I decided when I was little. What do you want for the cells you gave me? Is it better to be burned to ashes, or rot in the ground?"

I shake my head. I guess it doesn't matter once you're

dead. It only matters before you die, the way you imagine eternity in your head. "Whatever."

"Part of me will live on. In you, Josh. They can't kill the part of me that's you. And if I was meant to live, someone else must have been meant to die." He shrugs. "And they did."

Dad shakes his head. "I don't believe this. What the hell do you believe in? How could you decide to take someone else's life—"

"Decide? You believe in free will now?" Max says, without sparing Dad a glance. "The behavioral expert? Why do you assume it's something I *decided* to do?"

"Why, Max?" Dad says. He leans forward. "Help me understand, son. We want to help you, you know that. We'll get you the best doctors there are. Why did you do it? If it wasn't a decision, what made you do it? Can you understand it? Can you explain it?"

Max keeps staring at me even while he talks to Dad. I feel like a mouse caught in a trap. Helpless. Almost dead. "Well, you should find out in a few years if my DNA made me do it."

"Don't buy into your own press," Dad snaps. "You're no more alike than identical twins are. Less, since you were born at different times. Josh isn't you."

"I've been doing a lot of reading in here. The Bible, for instance. Josh, you know the story of Cain and Abel?"

"Yes. Yeah." I have to say it twice. The first time my throat is too dry for the sound to emerge. I don't know a lot of Bible stories, but I do know that one. "They were brothers. Cain killed Abel."

"Why?"

"He was jealous."

"Do you know why he was jealous?"

"I don't remember."

"God liked Abel better. Cain worked just as hard, tried just as hard to please God, but still, God liked Abel better. Not fair, is it?"

Dad covers his face with his hands. "So now you're Cain?"

"I don't know. Maybe I'm Abel. After all, he was the one who pleased God with his blood sacrifice. What do you think, Josh?"

What I think is that I hate Max. I hate him so much. Anger burns bright in my chest, then wanes. His eyes are brown, with a bit of green. Just like mine. Maybe he's thinking the same thing right now.

"Don't make a mess of your life, baby boy," he says softly, looking away. He shimmers back into my brother, and when the monster is no longer there, I feel bad about my hatred.

"I won't."

He grins at me when I meet his eyes again. "Don't get caught."

The chair falls over and bangs on the floor as I storm toward the door. I have to wait forever while the guard unlocks it and lets me out, and all the while, I can feel Max looking at me.

I hate him, I hate him, I hate him.

Seventeen

Our street is chaos. Cars and the television trucks and throngs of people. Dad veers away, taking another route through the neighborhood. He sighs.

"Maybe we should just check into a hotel or something," Mom whispers. "Or our offices . . . or Diane's house . . ."

"No," Dad barks. "We're not letting these vultures drive us out of our own home. Josh, get down on the floor."

"What?"

"Down," he insists. "We don't need to give them the satisfaction of getting your picture. They already have enough of those, thanks to your . . . thanks to Lione."

"Please, Jack. I didn't know," Mom says. "How could I have known? I thought he'd use those pictures to help Max."

"Never mind," Dad says. "Nothing we can do about it. Josh, down. Now!"

I undo my seat belt and slide down on the floor, lie face up, blinking at the beige ceiling. Mom throws a blanket on top of me, but through the coarse brown material, I still see the bright flashes of the cameras when we approach our house, hear the yelling of the reporters as we drive through the throng, hear Dad curse under his breath and Mom's labored breathing. I don't move at all until the garage door has closed behind us.

Mom puts her hand on my shoulder after I've thrown the blanket aside and gotten out of the car. "We need to talk, honey," Mom says. "We really need to talk about everything that's happened. . . ."

"I just want to be alone," I say, bite it out from my clenched jaw, shrug her hand off my shoulder. "I'm sick and tired of talking. I want to go to my room and I just want to be left alone."

"Josh, please . . ."

"Let him go," Dad says. "Give him space. We'll be here, Josh. When you're ready."

I go to my room and shut the door. My phone is ringing, all the phones are ringing. Reluctantly I check who it is. Frankie.

It rings for a long time, and in the end I answer.

"Is it true?" Frankie asks. "Are you okay?"

"Fine," I say stiltedly.

"Does it . . . do you . . . do they . . ." he stutters, and I can hear he doesn't know what to say. I don't help him out. I hold the phone to my ear with one hand, switch on my computer with the other, and just wait for him to finish his sentence. "Maybe I could come over?" he says at last. "We could . . . just hang out . . . you know?"

I roll my eyes, imagining Frankie strutting through the

crowd of hungry tyrannosaurs out there. But still, he's my friend. I think. I'm not sure I have a lot of friends left. "I don't think so. Maybe later. Not now."

"Why not? I mean, I won't talk about Max or anything. I won't go into his room. We could just, you know, hang out and—"

"Frank!" I hear Frankie's mom hissing at him. Then an inaudible mumble.

"Okay, see you later, got to go," Frankie says quickly, and hangs up.

I throw my phone hard against the wall. It bounces off and lands on my beanbag. I turn my back on it, go online, and log on to Genesis Alpha with my secondary character to avoid my friends. I'm trying not to think about me and Max, the reporters outside, the laboratory where they created me, but it's all so big it fills my entire brain. After a few minutes I quit and log on to some news sites. I'm everywhere. My picture and Max's side by side. Debates, profiles, interviews. One of the news stations even has a poll: "Will Max Seville's clone grow up to be a psychopath?"

There are 73 percent who say yes.

I keep searching the Internet for my name. It's everywhere. News, blogs, message boards. Still I don't realize just how big this is until I hear the noise outside. I go into Max's room and carefully peek past the curtains. More people. Even more cameras. And above, the noise I heard but couldn't place. A helicopter, hovering over our house.

I rush downstairs. Mom and Dad are in Dad's office. Dr.

Ashe is there too. They sit there together, all three of them, just like they did back when they plotted to create me.

I glare at her. "Dr. Frankenstein, I presume?"

"Hello, Josh," she says quietly.

"Here for visiting rights with your monster?"

"Cut it out, Josh." Dad doesn't even raise his voice at me. "I know everything seems overwhelming right now. And you have every right to feel betrayed. But this isn't the big issue you think it is."

"If this is no big deal, why is a helicopter circling our house?" I yell.

"Because the media has become a carnival," Dad shouts back. "Because the world has gone crazy. Because people are just as superstitious and ignorant now as they were back in the Dark Ages. You are not your brother. Of course you're not. Why not just burn us all at the stake?"

Dad is an idealist. He probably would have made a good hippie, but he was a generation late.

He's right, though. I saw that much on the Internet. Some people even think Max and I must share a soul. I guess they think God just makes one soul for each combination of DNA. If I had been the killer instead of Max, that would have made it even easier for them. They could claim I'd become a killer because I lacked a soul, that they'd created a body and a mind without a soul. Some will probably say it's the other way around, that I stole Max's soul and that's why he's evil.

"I'm sorry, Josh," Dr. Ashe says. Her voice is low. It always is. She sounds old and tired.

"People think I'll turn into Max," I say.

"They're wrong. They're ignorant." Dr. Ashe looks at my parents. "Could I talk to Josh alone for a minute?"

My parents hesitate but leave the room. I get that claustrophobic feeling I always get when I'm alone with Dr. Ashe. I try to face her but realize I'm shuffling my feet. "Why do you need to talk to me alone?"

"I thought you might have some questions. That you'd feel freer to ask them if your parents weren't here."

I should have questions. Just minutes ago I was filled with questions. But somehow I can think of only one that matters. My throat tightens as I force the words through. "Will I be like Max?"

Dr. Ashe pushes the glasses up her nose. "Do you remember the file cabinet under the window in my office?"

I picture her office in my mind. I've been there often enough. A huge desk, crammed with towering piles of papers and two computer screens. A photograph of her daughter, forever three years old, bald and laughing, between the two screens. A table and two chairs by a window. That's where I'd sit during tests. File cabinets. There is a tall file cabinet by the door, and a low one under the window. "Yeah. Is my file in there?"

"That cabinet is your file. Yours and Max's. Your intelligence tests, personality tests, neurological tests, your brain scans—it's all in there." She removes her glasses, rubs her eyes. "I tested Max until he was fourteen. After that, he wouldn't do it anymore."

"And?"

"You're very much alike," she says. "Your IQ profiles, your personality profiles, developmental stages, even your interest fields—very similar. That's normal for monozygotic twins, which is, essentially, what you are. But similar, Josh, is not identical."

"Could you tell? About Max? When he was my age?"

Dr. Ashe shakes her head. "I found nothing abnormal about Max at fourteen. Not that my tests could detect, that is."

"Are there tests that can detect things like that?"

"There are all sorts of tests. Questionnaires, even brain scans. They may tell you, statistically, whether you have what they call psychopathy or sociopathy or antisocial personality, but none of that matters, Josh. What matters is what you do. What you choose to do. Even if your tests results were identical to Max's, that wouldn't mean you'd ever do anything like what Max did. No test will tell you if you're likely to become a murderer."

"You said brain scans. What kind of a brain scan?"

"Psychopaths may have different brain responses from the rest of us. For example, most of us show a distinct reaction to disturbing photographs or words. You know, violent pictures, or words like 'blood' or 'rape' or 'death.' Psychopaths don't. For them, these words are like any other words."

"So you mean it isn't their fault? It's their brain? They can't help being wired like that?"

"Not all psychopaths choose to kill. Very few of them do, in fact. Some become very successful in competitive fields where a certain amount of ruthlessness pays off. And to approach it in reverse—many murderers are not psycho-pathic. It's not black and white, Josh. Not even close."

"Why do you say 'choose'? How can that be a choice? How can you not know the difference between right and wrong? And how can you know what's right and what's wrong, and not care?"

Dr. Ashe tries to smile. "You're moving into philosophy now. Not quite my field."

"If I take all the tests, the brain scan and everything, won't it tell me something? Won't it tell me something about what I am?"

She hesitates, then slowly shakes her head. "As a scientist, I would love to test you, because you're unique. But as a friend of your parents . . . as your friend, I hope—"

"You are not my friend!"

She continues like I haven't said anything. "What would be the point? Tests wouldn't tell you anything you need to know. Only you can tell yourself that."

My room is a mirror image of Max's room. It's across the hall from his, and my bed, my desk, my closets, everything's organized the same as his room. It's the way my parents arranged it when we were little, and although we both have different furniture now, everything is in the same place it always was.

It's time for a change.

I pull my desk across the room and push at my bed until it's on the other side of the window. My dresser goes into a corner, and I start to yank the drapes down but change my mind when I remember what's outside. There are identical drapes in Max's room, only a slightly different color. I'll get rid of them later.

It's stupid, really. Trying to change the small things, the insignificant things, when the real issue is inside me and will never change.

They can't look at me and say they know I'll never become that, do that. They can't know. Not when they watched Max grow up and become a monster behind their backs. That's the worst thing, perhaps. It's impossible to trust anything anymore. Although I look in the mirror and feel the same, I can't be sure what they see, and I can't trust what I see either.

I open the window, breathe in the cold air. This side of the house seems safe from reporters, at least for now. Rachel is still out there. She has no television, no radio, no Internet. Right now she's practically the only person in the world who doesn't know I'm a clone of Max.

I stare at the shed, trying to see a flicker of movement through the tiny windows, but they're narrow and small. She could probably turn cartwheels in there and I wouldn't see a thing.

The helicopter is gone now, but she must have noticed all the commotion. Must be wondering what's going on.

I see movement outside. I stare, worrying that it's a reporter. But it's only Dad, shuffling from the back door toward the shed.

I yank the window open. "Dad!" I call, and he stops, looks around.

"Josh?" he asks, finally looking up to my window.

"What are you doing?" I ask, breathless at the thought of Dad opening that door, of Rachel looking up, expecting me, and black upon black when my brain tries to imagine what comes next. "I'll clean the litter boxes. I always do, don't I? I'll do it tonight."

"Don't worry about it," Dad calls back to me. "I need something to do anyway." His hand is on the doorknob, and I'm practically hyperventilating. I do want Rachel to be found. I want her to go home. But not like this.

Dad disappears into the shed. My hands are clenched around the windowsill as I stand still, frozen, waiting for what comes next. But for long minutes there's nothing. Frantic, I bolt downstairs and rush out into the shed.

Dad is there. But Rachel isn't gone. He just hasn't noticed her. He's bent over the litter boxes and she's in the darkened corner, huddled up behind the paper box where the kittens lie. But one tiny squeak from a kitten and he'll look over there, and he'll see her.

"I told you I'd take care of this," Dad says, straightening up.

"I'll do it," I insist. "It's my chore."

Dad nods. He puts down the shovel and closes the cupboard, and I use the opportunity when his back is turned and push one of the blankets toward Rachel with my foot. She grabs it, drags it over herself. Even if he glances over there now, he probably won't notice anything out of the ordinary.

A kitten makes a tiny sound. Dad starts turning around, and I grab the box and push it toward him, making sure he keeps his back to Rachel. "Look. They were born yesterday," I say. Was it really only yesterday? It feels much longer. "Five of them."

"Yesterday?" Dad squats down for a look at the kittens. "You haven't mentioned them. Does your mom know?"

"No. She's got other things on her mind."

Dad grabs one of the huge boxes of cat litter, pulls it over, and sits down on it. He takes one of the kittens, holds it in his palms. "Josh . . . I know you said you wanted to be left alone . . . but is there anything you want to talk about now? Anything you want to ask?"

No. Absolutely not. Not here. Not with Rachel listening.

"I'm fine." I gesture toward the door. "I'll finish up here. You can go take care of Mom."

"She's all right. Diane's with her," he says, and doesn't budge.

"Let's go into the house and talk, then," I say.

Dad stares down at the kitten and doesn't move. "I've been thinking. It's probably best if we move away. And until we sell the house, maybe you could stay with your grandparents. A new school, a fresh start."

"I'll be fine. I don't want to go away." I walk toward the door. If I leave, Dad will shut up. He won't say anything about what I am.

I hope.

"This is a big story for the media, Josh," Dad says, just as I push at the door. "Not just the local press. Not just national press. This is international news. Historic news. And if you think the ethical debate over designer babies can be harsh . . ." He puts the kitten down, and I hold my breath, knowing what's coming. ". . . it's nothing compared to how people feel about clones."

Eighteen

There is no movement in the corner. I must have flinched, because my dad stands up and moves toward me. He puts his hands on my shoulders and makes me look at him. "Some people—ignorant people—are going to think this means you're another Max. Or that you aren't a real person. Or even something worse. It's a brutal world, Josh. I'm so sorry." Dad looks away. He draws his hand across his eyes.

When he looks back at me, there are tears in his eyes. "I'm sorry, son. At the time, I didn't think about you. What this would mean for you. What this would do to you. I thought of you as Max's cure, not as a real person. But I held you just after you were born, and I stared at you and you looked back at me, and I didn't remember you were Max's cure. I didn't even remember that they needed the cells from your umbilical cord until the doctor reminded me. I forgot about Max."

He slides back down on the box and rests his face in his hands. "And there's my guilt too. After you were born, when I held you, for a moment I forgot about Max."

■ ■ ■

Eventually Dad leaves. I wait until I hear the back door close. The blanket doesn't move at all. I wait for several minutes, but when nothing happens I grab the edge and yank the blanket off her.

Rachel stares at me, and she reminds me of two things at once: a cornered animal, frightened out of its skull, and a furious predator, ready to pounce. Nothing moves except her eyes, following my every movement.

I turn away from her. Finish up the litter boxes in absolute silence and wonder if she'll ever speak again. Between us, the kittens whine for their mother.

"A clone," she says at last, slowly and contemplatively. "You're Rook's clone."

"I didn't know. I found out today."

"How could you not know? Don't you feel it?"

"What should I feel?"

Rachel shudders. "You're him. You're identical. How can you not feel it?"

"I'm not him."

"You look the same. You're just younger. When you're his age, you'll be exactly the same. Your brains must be identical too."

"No. That's not how it works."

"Really? Then how does it work?" Rachel asks sardonically.

"The person you become . . . the brain . . . the mind. It's a mixture of so many different things . . . it's not just the genes."

"You have the same genes, the same parents, the same home. You must be the same. How didn't you know? They didn't want to tell you, did they? They didn't want you to know you were him. They wanted you to think you were your own person, but you're not. You can't be. Can you?" Her voice is smug, excited, but trembling with uncertainty, too, almost like she doesn't quite believe what she's saying.

I think I know how she feels. Like she has found the missing piece of a puzzle, like she's cramming it into place whether it fits there or not. And I don't know. I don't know if it fits. I feel like I'm wrapped up in lies, like a cocoon, and the silver threads are tightening so I can barely breathe.

"It's obvious, isn't it?" Rachel whispers. "Now. Now it's obvious. Because you look the same. You're a bit younger, that's all. And you dress differently. Your hair is different. Why?"

I don't say anything. I can't move.

"Why? Don't you want to look like him?"

She wants me to confirm it, wants me to confirm that I don't want to be like Max, and then when I've made that confession, she'll tell me it's no use, I'm just like him and there's nothing I can do about it.

Max wasn't a killer when he was my age. So just because I haven't done anything yet, that doesn't mean I'm innocent.

I'm just elsewhere in time.

Rachel starts humming. She does that a lot. I never recognize the melody. I think it's something she makes up. It doesn't seem to mean anything either. She hums when she's playing with the cats, and when she's about to say something nasty, and when she gets that faraway look in her eyes and talks about her sister, and when she rocks backs and forth and carves bloody patterns into her skin.

"We learned about cloning in school," Rachel says. "They made you from him, didn't they? They took one of his cells, and they actually used it to create a copy of Rook. You're the copy. Correct?"

I try to ignore her.

"So you're like an extension of him. A body part, almost. His cell, instead of becoming a part of his liver or his ear or something, became you."

"Shut up."

"Why? It's the truth, isn't it?"

Rachel wants to hurt me. And I can't help feeling I deserve it. Max deserves to be hurt, but I don't think Rachel's words would hurt him. They do hurt me, though. That's probably a good thing.

"Only you accidentally got your own brain, too," Rachel continues mercilessly. "You didn't only provide him with those healing cells, you accidentally became your own person, with your own soul and everything. Or is it your own?"

Is it? Or am I Max?

Rachel has the knife in her hand. I fumble in my pockets, sure I'd left it there, but come up empty. She has stolen her knife back and is making tiny cuts to the back of her hand. Barely drawing blood. I lean over and snatch the knife from her. Close it. Put it in my pocket.

She tosses her hair. "Fine. More fingerprints. More of my blood on your hands. You're digging your own grave." She grins wider. "Or should I say, building your own electric chair? Mixing your own lethal injection?"

"Shut up."

She does. She lies there on the mattress, staring up, and doesn't say a thing. Neither do I.

Rachel's shoulders move, tremble as she draws in a breath. "If you could change the past, what's the one thing you would change?"

Would I cancel my birth? I like life. I want to be alive. Would it be possible for me to be alive, but for Karen not to have died?

"I'd want my brother not to be a killer," I say at last.

"No. It has to be something you could have changed. Something you could have done. Something that's in your power."

I search through all the things I'd like to change, but none of it was in my power. There's nothing I could have done to change what Max did.

"If I'd known Rook would kill Karen, I would have done something," Rachel says. "But I didn't know. I suspected he was bad news. But I didn't know. So I didn't do anything. But I still feel guilty. Because I suspected. It should have been enough."

She's pulling at her skin with her nails now. The backs of her hands are a mess. I stand up. I fling myself on the mattress next to her, cornering her off. She sucks in a breath, recoils.

I dig into my pocket for the knife, pull at the different tools until the right one emerges. Rachel sees the flash of metal in my hand. Her breath speeds up. I grab her wrist. Feel the fragile bones through her sweater, hold tight, even though she whimpers and scrambles backward until her back pushes into the corner. She's panting now, she's terrified, but I don't care, for a moment I even like it that she's scared. She gasps as I bring the knife to her hand, exhales sharply when I start cutting.

Her fingernails. They were once covered with pale pink polish, but most of it is gone. I cut them short, even shorter than mine.

"What are you doing?" Rachel asks when the third nail has been clipped, when it's obvious what I'm doing, but she doesn't yank her hand away, and I keep going. I cut all the nails, fling her hand away, and grab her other wrist.

Rachel stares at her hands when I'm done. Holds them out like girls do when they're admiring their nails. "This won't change anything, you know," she says conversationally. She flexes her hands, traces a finger over the nails on her right hand. "I can still use a knife. Or a rusty nail from the walls here. A shard of glass. I can use anything."

"Why do you do it?"

"I don't know."

"Karen didn't cut herself."

"No. She didn't have to. Rook did it for her."

Before I can say anything, the door slams open. A figure shuffles in, brushing the snow off his hair. "Your dad told me you'd be here. . . . Man, do you know there was a helicopter circling your—"

Frankie stops short. He stares at us, his hand still in his hair. Melted snow leaks down into his sleeve as he stands there, and time slows down.

He sees Rachel. That's the first thing I think. In a way I'm relieved. She can't hide here anymore after Frankie knows she's here. Frankie's not exactly good at keeping secrets.

But then I see the look on his face. I see him recognize Rachel. I see him turn his head to me, look at the knife I'm still holding in my hand. I see his eyes widen. Then he twirls back. Droplets of melted snow shoot off him and hit me in the face. The door slams shut behind him.

I hear him scream for help.

And Rachel starts laughing.

Nineteen

Rachel's still laughing when she grabs my arm, pulls me out of the shed. "Come on!" she says, running, her hand tight around mine. She's heading toward the forest that hugs our backyard, and we run together, like a three-legged race. She's holding on to my hand, nothing else, yet I feel like we're bound together, like I can't help but run with her.

It's stupid. It's so stupid. The last thing I should be doing now is running away. But I allow her to drag me into the forest, we're running in random twists and turns between the silent trees. I'm only wearing shoes, not boots, and my feet quickly get soaked from running in the snow. It's quiet in here, all I hear is our harsh breathing and our feet hitting the ground. Quiet and white. The branches are heavy with snow, and there's still some coming down, but the weather has been getting warmer, so everywhere water drips from above, almost like rain. It will be easy to track us, I think, looking back at the trail we leave.

A phone rings. The cheery tune doesn't belong here, but I

recognize it. Mine. I dig my phone out of my pocket, look at the display. Dad. I answer.

Rachel stops. She leans back against a tree and looks at me, her thumbnail in her mouth.

"Josh?" Dad's voice is anxious. "What's going on?"

"Nothing."

"Frankie told us there was a girl with you out in the shed."

"So?"

"Nothing. It's okay. You can have friends over, you know that. But . . . he thinks . . . Frankie thinks it's the missing Crosse girl. Karen Crosse's sister."

I look at Rachel, and she stares back at me. "Yes. He's right."

Dad hesitates. *Frankie says you had a knife.* I know that's what he thinking. But he doesn't say it.

"Where are you? Why did you run off? Is the girl still with you?"

"Yes, she's here. Her name is Rachel."

"Put her on the phone, please. I'd like to talk to her."

I clench my hand around the phone until the plastic creaks. "Why? To ask if I'm holding her captive? To check if I've cut her face yet? To see if she's still alive?"

"Josh. Don't do this. Frankie has already called the police. I can hear the sirens."

"Rachel is here. She's fine. I'm taking her home."

I hang up and turn the phone off. Rachel gnaws on her nail, looks at me skeptically. "You're taking me home? You and what army?"

"Why did you drag me out here?"

She shrugs. Clenches her fists, pulls her arms up, so her sleeves hang empty. "I don't know. I just wanted . . . I didn't want to wait there. For people to barge in. Police and stuff. My parents. I'm not . . . ready. I needed to think."

"You want to get me in trouble," I growl at her. "You want to show them I'm like Max."

"Are you?"

There's a burning sensation in my throat, tickling my nose. I won't cry in front of Rachel. I scoop some snow off the ground and spend several seconds sculpting a perfect snowball. I stretch my arm back and throw it with all my force. It splatters against the tree trunk three feet above Rachel's head and disintegrates. Snow rains down on her, but she doesn't seem to notice. She doesn't notice the hard snowball hurled in her direction, the tree shaking from the impact, the fragments plunging down on her head. She just stands there, looking small, and waits for my answer.

"Yes," I say. "I'm a lot like him. And it scares me. I'm scared . . ." I bite my lip and can't believe I said that. Rachel has enough ammunition without me handing her another crate of grenades.

Rachel's hair is windblown and her cheeks red from our run. She looks different outside. More like a normal person. "He's not," she says slowly, like she's still thinking her words through while she speaks.

"He's not what?"

"He's not scared to be what he is. He wants to be that way. Doesn't he?"

I see Max's face. No guilt, no regret. Only annoyance and anger. Frustration—and fear for his own life. "Yeah. I guess. He doesn't care what he did. He just regrets that he got caught. He feels sorry for himself, not for anyone else. He doesn't feel sorry for Karen. Or for . . ." I stop, because self-pity is pathetic.

"You?"

"Come on. Let's go. I'll take you home."

Rachel doesn't budge. "What's going to happen to us?" she asks. "To you? What happens to clones of killers?"

"I don't know."

"Will you move away? Change your name?"

"Maybe."

Rachel nods. "That might be a good idea. Maybe. But maybe not. You'd always have something to hide. You'd go to college and graduate and get a job. You'd meet a girl and get married and have kids, and have this whole fantastic life. Then one day you'd wake up to the same headline, and you'd lose everything. It's better, isn't it, that people know up front?"

"I guess. Maybe."

"You're not that much like him, you know."

I'm ice inside. But a little sliver thaws, jolting my heart, and I feel it beating for the first time in ages. Still I shrug, because I don't trust Rachel. She may be taunting me. Setting me up. Patting my cheek before slashing it with a knife.

"He'll haunt you forever," Rachel says. "Won't he?"

"Yeah."

She sighs. Leans back against the tree, then slides down to sit there in the snow, looks up at the winter sky through the crown of naked branches. "Me too. I don't even want him dead. I'm scared. I'm scared he'll haunt me." Her lips tremble. "Isn't it silly? I don't believe in ghosts, but I want him there, locked away, not dead so that his spirit can pass through the prison walls. I can't sleep when I think about him being a ghost."

If I don't get you in this life, I will in the next.

"I know."

"What if they could give Rook a soul transfusion?" Rachel asks. "If they could kill all the evil in him, just like they killed the cancer, and replace it with good? Would you give him a part of your soul?"

"There is no such thing as a soul transfusion."

"If there was. If his evil were a cancer of his soul, and he needed a new one. Would you give him a part of yours?"

"How would my soul help, if it's just like his?" I growl.

"Have you ever killed someone?"

"Don't be stupid."

"Have you?"

"No!"

"Not even in a computer game?"

"Of course. You know that. You play too. I've killed inside a computer game a million times. That doesn't count."

"Why not?"

I look up and sigh. "Because it's a game. They aren't real people. They were programmed to be killed. They don't have a soul or a mind or feelings or anything. And they re-spawn. They don't drop down and are dead forever."

"Maybe it's all the same to Rook. Computer creatures and real people, he doesn't think there is a difference."

"I don't know."

If we don't have free will, Max isn't evil. It isn't his fault. It's just the way he was made.

But then I would be the same. Wouldn't I?

There has to be an explanation, a reason, an answer. Everybody keeps asking, but no one is answering. Not really.

What if I'd been in Max's place, and he in mine? Would I be the killer then?

There is no answer. No satisfactory solution.

I want to believe in free will. I want to believe Max chose to do what he did. I want to believe that he chose to ruin lives—including his own. But why would he choose something like that?

Why did he do it? Because he wanted to?

Why? Because he had to?

Why? Because . . .

It scares me that I can't get to the end of "why." It scares me because it means there isn't an answer to "why not," either—no guarantee that I'm not like Max. No guarantee, except that I know now what people can do, what people like Max can do, what people like me can do. At least that much I've learned from Max.

"Your dad—he said people would think you were just like him. That they were ignorant. Do you think he's right?"

I don't know. Maybe they're not superstitious at all. Maybe they know that DNA is only a blueprint or a recipe, not all we are. But they may also believe the evil in Max is an end product that will always push through. Like a blueprint for a car can never become a house, and a recipe for bread can never become a salad. "I don't know," I say. "Maybe he's wrong. Maybe they're right. Maybe you're right."

Rachel holds out her hand and I grab it, pull so she can stand up. She doesn't let go of my hand, but opens my palm, presses our fingers together. My hand is much bigger than hers. My hands are like Max's hands.

She turns my palm up and traces my fingertips. "Your fingerprints are different from his," she says. "I remember that from biology class. Identical twins have different fingerprints. So do clones."

"Yes."

"Your mind is different too."

It's what I told her. It's what I want her to believe. It's what I want to believe. "I can't be sure."

"Why not?"

"It's Max's genes. I was made from what he is. It's like . . . It's like Max is there. Inside me. Looking out through my eyes. Yanking my thoughts around. Like in Genesis Alpha. Like he's the player, the real person, and I'm just the character. I'll never get him out of my head. He's a part of me. But it's different for you. You can get rid of him. You don't have to carry him inside your head forever."

Rachel releases me. She pushes her hands deep into the pockets of her jeans. "If you fire a gun often enough at a ghost, will it die?"

I don't answer.

"It will never be over. Not for me, either. Even if they kill him, he'll never die. He'll be every guy who smiles at me. He'll be every footstep behind me when I'm walking somewhere alone. He'll be every knock on the door late at night. He'll be every person I meet online. He'll be a ghost at my heels for the rest of my life. And I don't know if I can exist in that kind of a world." She looks at me, and rare tears glisten in her eyes. "I see him everywhere, Josh. Everywhere. But I don't see him in your face. Not in your eyes. Not anymore."

I look away, but breathing is slightly easier. Like gravity just let up a bit.

"I didn't realize it until I heard you were his clone. I should see him in you now, more than ever. And I looked. I looked at you and I expected to see Rook. But I didn't. He isn't there. You're not him."

I'm like a book, Mom once explained to me when she helped with my biology homework. My story, like everybody's story, is made up of letters. ACGT. The four chemicals making up our DNA. Just four letters standing for everything we are.

Max's book and mine are the same. Every letter in the same place. Every letter identical.

Could we still become two different stories?

"I'm going home now," Rachel says.

"Will you be okay?"

"I don't know."

I kick at the snow, keep my eyes on the ground. "The kittens will be ready for new homes soon."

When I look up, Rachel is smiling. It's an unusually small smile. Doesn't remind me of a rubber mask this time. "Yes. Prince. Princess. The boy, and the blue girl."

"You can have them. In the spring, they'll be ready."

Rachel nods. She pushes away from the tree and grabs my hand, like before, when she dragged me through the snow. I feel one of the scars in her palm push at my skin, but as my hand gets used to holding hers, I stop noticing. Then she lets go, and we just walk, our hands swinging by our sides, almost touching.

"Will you keep playing Genesis Alpha?" Rachel asks when we're nearly all the way back. Blue blinking lights smear the air long before we see the house. There are people all over our yard, three men are advancing through the forest toward us.

"I don't know."

"It's not the game's fault. It's a good game. It's not its fault what Rook used it for. Maybe someday we could play together."

I look cautiously at her face. I don't trust her. When we get back, she may tell the police lies, show them her bruises and cuts and tell them I inflicted them. "Sure."

She smiles as three police officers come running toward us. Two of them have actually drawn their guns and are pointing them at us. At me.

"Good," she says, stopping. She nods toward the yelling police officers and puts her hands up, like in the movies. Feeling totally silly, I do the same. "Someday. We'll play."

Twenty

After midnight, when chaos has retired for the night—Rachel has gone home, the police have gone without cuffing me, the throng outside has thinned to a couple of desperate reporters, and my parents have settled down to something close to their normal level of confusion and misery—I turn on my computer and log on to Genesis Alpha. I'm not sleepy. I'm not sure I'll ever be tired again.

My hand moves slowly over the keyboard. One letter at a time.

Rook2King.

MyPAzw3rd.

Then I take a deep breath and click login.

"Account closed—Character deleted" appears on my screen. Then small print about contacting user support if there's a problem.

Rook is gone. The police have had his account closed. I should have guessed.

I stare at the words for a while.

They're wrong. He's not gone. Not completely.

In my pocket, the knife seems almost to pulse. Rook's there. I made a copy and saved him. He's still there.

I plug the knife into the computer. Uploading to the regular game won't work with the account gone, so instead I upload Rook to the test server. Then I delete the files from the knife, overwrite them with random system files, unplug the knife, and toss it across the room. Gone.

And Rook's standing on his mountaintop again, looking out over the world.

Good and evil is easy in Genesis Alpha. It's a simple continuum, not a four-dimensional maze like the real world. The game defines which actions are good and which are bad, and it's all very predictable. You can kill as much as you want, as long as you kill "bad" creatures or "bad" players. Do lots of good things, and you're good. Do lots of bad things, and you're bad. Do a mixture of good and bad, and you're neutral.

In the real world, everybody knows what's good or bad— mostly. It gets complicated, of course, but for most things, most of the big things, you just know what's right and what's wrong. You don't have to think about it a lot, you just know. Something inside tells you.

Max knows. Max knows killing is wrong. He knows, but he doesn't care.

I care.

It's not possible to fix what Max did. Not in the real world. But in Genesis Alpha, many good things can balance out the evil. Do enough good, and even the most evil player eventually becomes good.

I move Rook around. Manipulate him at will. I make him run, turn him in circles, look at him from all angles. Make him jump, fall, laugh, cry.

I could turn Rook good. I could play him for a while, could take him out on missions, make him rescue the weak, kill the bad guys, and in time, he would become good. If I kept making him do only good things, a soft light aura would emerge around his player portrait, until he's standing in a pool of light.

I could do that. I could turn Rook good.

But there is no point. Not really. It doesn't change what Max did. There is no redemption for that.

I park the spaceship on a primitive planet and walk Rook into a green alley nestled between tall mountains. He has no sword, no armor. He's been here before. He has enemies who'll remember him.

On my screen, little people come running from all directions. They remember Rook. I override his automatic command to fight back. It isn't easy. The program kicks in every few seconds, ordering him to fight back, to defend himself. I have to keep ordering him to stand still.

The crowd keeps growing. They are little people, gnomes. An easy kill for a strong player like Rook. All he needs to do is pull his sword, and several of them would fall from one slash through the crowd.

But he doesn't have a sword. Not even a pocketknife. Nothing. I don't even allow him to fight back with his fists.

I watch his hit points indicator. He's hardly taking any hits at all. And he heals automatically, too. I know he's just a computer character and that he's now under my control, but when I look at his face on the screen, I can almost sense his frustration, his anger at what I'm doing to him—and his gloating over how strong and invincible he is, that even alone, unarmored, the dozens of creatures can't bring him down.

One by one, the hit points drain away from him, but he keeps healing to make up for it. I watch for a while as his hit points inch downward, then jerk upward again as healing kicks in. I almost hear him laugh at me. He won't die. He'll never die. Not like this. It will take something much bigger to kill him.

I hit the off button. Press it with my thumb, hold it.

The computer whines in protest.

The screen goes blank.

Inside the game, standing there in the middle of the gnome swarm, Rook has turned into a statue. The gnomes will lose interest and leave. He'll be left there alone, and the statue will grow mossy and moldy. In time it will decay and crumble.

Rook's gone. He will never return to Genesis Alpha.

His game is over.

Mine's not.